The yellowbacks... classics of popular fiction

The yellowjackets or yellowbacks were a great series of bestselling adventure and crime thrillers that had its origins in the mid to late 19th century following on from the 'penny dreadfuls'. They virtually began the mass market revolution of the early 20th century with a clear standard format and imprint/series livery (what would today be called branding). Hodder & Stoughton published the yellowjackets in two main series with series run dates of: 1923-1939 and later 1949-1957.

As the tagline ('where thrillers really began') on the back cover implies, the imprint and series focused on thrillers that were the bestsellers of their time. This current reissue or retro revival if you will, brings back many of these masterpieces, now classics in their own way and extends it further by including key titles from that period that were either great crime or thriller or even general commercial fiction (including sub-genres of noir, horror, gothic, romance, westerns, etc.) influences of their time. There are some perennial favourites and many rarities either lost or not easily available being revived in the current series. Writers and characters ranged from adventure heroes like Bulldog Drummond, Allan Quatermain, Richard Hannay or the Saint through thriller grandmasters Edgar Wallace and E. Phillips Oppenheim, crime and mystery maestros like Patricia Wentworth, GK Chesterton, Agatha Christie and the Detection club, to western and swashbucklers like Zane Grey, Max Brand, Captain Blood and even romance or general fiction classics like Hermina Black, Denise Robins, Marie Corelli or Stella Morton. These were books that had storytelling at their heart and always entertained.

The yellowbacks had both hardback (with varying design elements) and paperback (which built the series look) versions with the latter still carrying the imprint 'yellowjacket'. The current reissues pay tribute to both and use an amalgam of elements from both editions while retaining the complete yellow (or 'mustard-plaster') livery with the author's name in blue beveled type with a 'simulated emboss' effect and a white outer 'outline', and the book title in black. These reissues retain the distinctive size of the original mass market paperback and follow the three main category variations—the thrillers (crime, westerns, mystery, adventure) had blue lettering for the author's name, while Romance and softer general fiction had red; and other categories like humour had green.

For more detail and a full list of titles visit https://www.hachetteindia.com/home/yellowbacks

THE MEMOIRS OF
CONSTANTINE DIX

THE MEMOIRS OF CONSTANTINE DIX

Barry Pain (1864 – 1928) was born in Cambridge, and educated at Sedbergh School and Corpus Christi College, Cambridge. He became a prominent contributor to *The Granta*. He was known as a writer of parody and lightly humorous stories.

In 1889, Cornhill Magazine's editor, James Payn, published his story 'The Hundred Gates', and shortly afterwards Pain became a contributor to *Punch* and *The Speaker*, and joined the staffs of the *Daily Chronicle* and *Black and White*. Pain supposedly "owes his discovery to Robert Louis Stevenson, who compares him to De Maupassant". From 1896 to 1928, he was a regular contributor to *The Windsor Magazine*. He died in Bushey, in Hertfordshire on 5 May 1928.

THE
MEMOIRS OF
CONSTANTINE DIX

Barry Pain

The Memoirs of Constantine Dix
First Published by T. Fisher Unwin, London in 1905

This Hodder Yellowback edition © Hachette India 2023
(Registered Name: Hachette Book Publishing India Pvt. Ltd.)
An Hachette UK Company www.hachetteindia.com

1

All rights reserved. No part of the publication may be reproduced, stored in a retrieval system (including but not limited to computers, disks, external drives, electronic or digital devices, e-readers, websites), or transmitted in any form or by any means (including but not limited to cyclostyling, photocopying, docutech or other reprographic reproductions, mechanical, recording, electronic, digital versions) without the prior written permission of the publisher, nor be otherwise circulated in any form of binding or cover other than that in which it is published and without a similar condition being imposed on the subsequent purchaser.

The texts in these editions in most cases have been reprinted as is, with minimal editorial changes and by and large no bowdlerizing for political correctness; though in some editions, a few words and phrases considered archaic, or those considered offensive now, along with archaic punctuation may have been modified in places to make the text more accessible to today's readers. The narratives, language, beliefs, social mores and/or cultural depictions, in these volumes are a reflection of their times and must be viewed as such. They may also contain certain cultural, racial and gender prejudices and stereotypes that may be outdated or clearly wrong then and wrong today; but their removal would be tantamount to claiming these prejudices never existed. The Publisher does not endorse or support those depictions or stereotypes; and these books have been made available for a discerning audience that will read it for entertainment value and a chronicle/record of popular fiction of past times.

Cover design by Priya Singh adapted from the original classic yellowjacket by Hodder & Stoughton.

Cover illustration by Ishan Trivedi.

Series note: Some of the books in the series (unless otherwise credited) may have cover or inside illustrations from the original yellowbacks or early editions, and while full restoration has been attempted, some images may be grainy or faded due to the condition of the original material. The end notes or bonus material or blurb details may have been sourced from the public domain or free use publications such as Wikipedia and attribution is hereby made also allowing similar free use reproduction from here. Sources requiring further specific attribution may write in and further detailing and/or corrections shall be made in subsequent printings/editions.

Reprint specifications may be subject to change including but not limited to finishes, paper, colour sections.

ISBN: 978-93-5731-039-0

Hachette Book Publishing India Pvt. Ltd.
4th & 5th Floors, Corporate Centre,
Plot No. 94, Sector 44, Gurugram - 122 003, India

Typeset in Electra LT STD 10/12.5 pt by Manipal Technologies Limited, Manipal

Printed and bound in India by Manipal Technologies Limited, Manipal

CONTENTS

I.	The Dead Man Wins	1
II.	Reclamation Work	11
III.	With A Clear Conscience	22
IV.	Checkmate	33
V.	The Rewards of Perseverance	42
VI.	Lost Property	54
VII.	Holiday Work	64
VIII.	The Bellasen Cross	73
IX.	Numbered Notes	87
X.	Impersonation	96
XI.	The Change	104
XII.	Murder	117

I

THE DEAD MAN WINS

Bingham sacked his third footman. The fellow had got as drunk as an owl, and had been insolent. He had no character, and he was a fool; so he came to London. There he hung about the docks, and spent what little money he had, and got into bad company. Ikey got hold of him. One night when Ikey had nothing better to do, he made the idiot drunk, and while he was drunk he told the plain truth about Bingham and the diamonds. I heard of it from Ikey the next day, when he had found religion and wanted to lead quite a new life. I am glad to say that I had friends who put him in the way of some honest work. The information about Bingham, I thought, would be of use to me.

If you enquire at Scotland Yard, where my name is known, they will tell you that I am engaged in rescue work, and do a lot of good. They will probably add that I have independent means, and am frequently imposed upon. It may be so. I am not at all anxious that Scotland Yard should change its mind on the subject.

I am not attached to any particular denomination, but I trust that I am sympathetic with all of them. The Catholics have great hopes of winning me in the end; so also have the Nonconformists. Many an Anglican clergyman has told me that he wished the Church included in its fold more such workers as myself. I go about a great deal among the criminal classes in the poorest part of London. I give them not only excellent advice and spiritual consolation, but material help in money or food when times are bad, and sometimes I hear of things from them which I think are likely to be useful, as in the case of that little information about Bingham.

I am also, as you may have conjectured, a thief. I have been a thief for many years. I have never been in prison, and I do not propose to go there. It is not really necessary if one will only follow a few simple rules. To begin with, I have never in my life possessed anything which the police would call a housebreaking implement. Explanation of one's presence uninvited in another man's house at midnight is only rendered more difficult if a box of silent matches, a jemmy, a drill and a revolver are found in one's possession. Without such tools it is impossible to attempt the opening of a good safe; but I never attempt the opening of a good safe. My pocket-knife contains all the tools that I require; and the place of a revolver is taken by what appears to be a simple cigarette. When I am taken I trust I shall behave civilly and like a gentleman; and I have no doubt that the officer will permit me one last smoke on my way to the station. Then that cigarette will come in, and that officer and myself will get a pretty object-lesson in the use of high explosives. Unfortunately we shall not live to profit by it. I have never had a confederate and I very rarely make use of a receiver; the only receiver whom I ever used lives in Brussels, does not know my right name and address, is under the impression that I am a diamond merchant, and would not dream of receiving stolen goods if he knew that he were doing so. It is a rule of my life that the successful thief must in all possible respects live like an honest man. No dishonesty except on business. I have twice found valuable property in the street, and on both occasions I took it to Scotland Yard.

I am one of the few persons now living who have never attempted to cheat a railway company. I never avoid the police, and they are happily convinced of my philanthropic motives in associating with bad characters. I never drink intoxicating liquor unless I mean to get intoxicated. This simple rule alone would have saved many men the sacrifice of their freedom. I do not believe in unnecessary risks, cumbersome loot, numbered notes, overruling ambitions or extravagance in living. If it is objected to me that I only go for the soft things, my vanity is not wounded, and my common-sense is complimented. I am investing my money as I make it, for I do not want to work all my life.

I am then a lay-preacher and an habitual thief. You will add that I am a hypocrite: frankly, I do not know whether I am or not. I speak the truth here; the publication of these memoirs can only occur when the truth can no longer injure me. And I say with truth that I am thoroughly in earnest in my rescue work. I have pleaded with these men with tears in my eyes; I have never preached without believing every word that I said. The police could point out to you men whom I have reformed—men who are now living honestly and in good positions through my help. I can help others but not myself. That I believe to be predestined. I accept the case as it is, and do not worry myself with introspection.

When Ikey (not for the first or second time) found religion he naturally came to me. He told me what he had heard from Bingham's dismissed servant, and admitted that but for his regeneration he would probably at that moment have been looking for Bingham's diamonds. He seemed very thankful, and his whole face was radiant. I regret to say about a year later he again fell into evil courses.

The story that Bingham's footman—his name was Evans—brought to Ikey was rather curious. Sir Charles Bingham, as everybody knows, made his money in South Africa. His house at Weybridge was interesting, and stood in picturesque grounds. Bingham was rather proud of the place. He was at this time a man of forty and unmarried. He was fond of entertaining, and generally had visitors in the house while he was there. In the dining-room the service door was screened off by a tall, four-fold leather screen. One night, after dinner, the butler stood behind that screen, and heard what Bingham was saying to one of his guests. It was nice useful information, and the butler acted upon it next day. The shares went up with a rush, the butler retired on his profits, and Evans got to hear about it. After that Evans used to be rather fond of standing unseen behind that leather screen when the ladies had gone and the men were talking. He heard a good deal. He acquired quite a collection of humorous, though slightly indelicate stories, but he never heard Sir Charles say anything was good to buy for a quick rise; possibly Sir Charles had his suspicions in the case of the butler.

One night Evans heard a guest (whom he always spoke of as the Colonel) say to Bingham:

"What about those diamonds? Got them here still?"

Sir Charles said he had.

"You'll lose them for a certainty," said the Colonel. "Why don't you send them to your banker, or at least keep them in a good strong safe?"

"I don't send them to the bank because I am interested in them, and I like to look at them. To my mind they are as pretty as flowers. I don't keep them in a safe because to do that would be practically to tell the burglar where to look for them, and the best safe is of no use against the cleverest burglar. My system is all right. At any rate I have not lost them yet."

"Where are they now?" the Colonel asked.

"In my pocket. You can have a look at them if you like."

Evans also would have liked—very much liked—to have had a look at them, but he dared not show his head round the edge of the screen. He could hear the crackle of paper being unfolded and murmurs of admiration and astonishment.

"And where will they be tonight?" said the Colonel.

"I shall hide them somewhere or other as usual. I am the last man to go to bed in this house, and as a rule I hide them just before going to bed. It's rather amusing to think of new places."

"It's absolutely childish," said the Colonel.

"How would you like me to go and look for them tonight?"

"You can if you like," said Sir Charles; "on one condition. They shall be hidden in a place accessible to you, and if you have got them at breakfast-time tomorrow you may keep them. If you have not got them you will pay me a sovereign."

"Good!" said the Colonel. "I think I would take five thousand to one about anything on the face of this earth. You will lose your diamonds tonight."

"Think so?" said Sir Charles, and changed the subject.

The Colonel did not go to bed that night. At breakfast-time he handed his host a sovereign, and was told where the diamonds had been hidden. They had been under the coals in the scuttle in the Colonel's bedroom.

Evans now felt that the diamonds were practically in his pocket. Every night he determined to hunt for them. Fortunately, or unfortunately for him, his elation and the strain on his nerves led him to drink, and before a week was over he had been dismissed.

This was the story that Ikey told me, and on the following day I bought a very nice hand-camera and went down to Weybridge.

I took a cab at Weybridge Station, and stopped in at the lodge to enquire if Sir Charles was likely to be at home. I then went on up to the house. I gave the butler my card with my correct name and address upon it. The commonest mistake that an uneducated thief makes is to use an *alias* when no *alias* is necessary. I asked the man to take my card to Sir Charles and request permission for an amateur to make one or two photographs in his grounds for a private collection. I waited in the big square hall. I had only waited two or three minutes before Sir Charles appeared; but I do not think the diamonds were hidden in the hall.

Sir Charles came out from the drawing-room. He was a big, fat, lazy-looking man, with his hands thrust into the pockets of his light Norfolk jacket. He seemed to be slightly annoyed—at which I was not surprised—and eyed me up and down quickly. He was an ugly man and seemed a strong man.

"Afternoon," said Sir Charles. "It's you that wants to photograph my place?"

"If you would be kind enough to give me permission."

"I say, you know, I never heard of such a thing! It's not for any paper, is it? They are always bothering me, and I won't have it—I simply won't have it. See?"

"I have no connection with the Press whatever. A friend of mine, General Tomlinson, came here some time ago to see you about a footman who had been in your employ—a man called Evans. You were away at the time but my friend noticed the remarkable beauty of the place, knowing my photographic hobby, and—"

Sir Charles broke in impatiently.

"Evans was a drunken scamp. I told him he would have no character, and it was no good to send anybody to me." But I could see that the appreciation of his place had moved him rather. "Still," he went on, "I don't know why you shouldn't photograph if you want to. It is rather a pretty spot, so they tell me. It's quite understood that it is simply for your own private collection."

"Certainly, Sir Charles, simply for that, though I should hope to have the pleasure of sending you copies of course."

"Thanks," said Sir Charles. He paused a moment irresolute, and then snatched up an aged Panama hat. "Come along," he said, "I'll show you some of the best bits."

I took two or three photographs in the garden, and afterwards some time-exposures of different rooms in the house. It was easy enough with a little more flattery to lead from the one thing to the other, in fact it was Sir Charles himself who suggested that I should photograph in the house. He became very civil, and wanted me to have a whiskey and soda with him before I went I refused of course. (The photographs turned out very well. I sent him a complete set of them afterwards, and he wrote and thanked me.) And as soon as I was safely back in my cab I drew from my pocket the wisp of green paper which I had taken from behind the tall clock in the dining-room. I unfolded it with the greatest care. It contained a few tin-tacks.

I confess to some slight feeling of disappointment—it was not irritation; I did not swear, and I may say here that I have never used a profane word in my life. I had not got the diamonds, but I had got a variety of useful information. I knew, for instance, that alarm guns were used, and I had been able to see where the wires were stretched at night on the lawn and across the drive. I also knew, for Sir Charles himself had told me, that he considered a holly hedge seven feet in height, and about three feet through, to be burglar-proof—which is not the case. The photographs which I had taken were themselves of use in enabling me to find my way about. So I was not impatient.

Having thought out my plan of action I went down to Weybridge about a week later. I had left my motor-car at Guildford with instructions that I should come up from London to fetch it early on the morning of the following day. I reached Weybridge at about seven in the evening and went straight to the fields at the back of Bingham's grounds. I examined the holly hedge, marked the best spot, and then went into the town to dine. I returned at ten, and got to work at once. I could see that there were still lights in the house, but I was out of sight and I made little or no noise. With the aid of the implements and my pocketknife I had by eleven o'clock made a hole in the hedge through which I could crawl. Holly is after all very easy to handle if you have intelligence and thick gloves. The full moon was now coming up, and I think I could have detected any of the wires, at any rate on the gravel. But as a measure of precaution I walked principally on the flower-beds; flowerbeds are never wired. There seems to be a prevalent belief that a burglar would hesitate to break a geranium or fuchsia. This is not the case. I walked round the house in safety till I got to the porch. I should imagine that this was ten or eleven feet high, with a square roof to it, supported on pillars. From the top of this porch access was easy to the window of a little room which Sir Charles had described to me as his own study. I had made a photograph of this room at his special request; it seemed to be his favourite room, and I thought there was a fair chance that here I should find the diamonds. In studying my photograph of the room I was particularly struck by a tall bookcase, reaching from floor to ceiling and covering the middle third of one of the walls. It occurred to me that Sir Charles Bingham might possibly consider the space behind the books to be a good hiding-place.

I had already examined the ladders and had found them extremely well chained and locked. The lock would have presented no great difficulty to me, but there was very likely some electrical alarm attached. The place where they were kept was suspicious, and I did not like it; so I left the ladders alone and trusted to my skill in throwing the noose and in climbing a rope to get me to the top of the porch. The rope I was carrying in a coil under my waistcoat. I succeeded at the first attempt in noosing a projection of the parapet that ran round the roof of the porch. Funnily enough, I did not like this; things were going too easily; that always makes me suspicious. However, up I went and tried the study window. It was bolted, and when I slipped my knife in and forced back the spring it went with a snap that might have aroused the seven sleepers. I lay flat on my face in the shadow and waited. I could not hear a sound, and not a glimmer of light appeared anywhere. Again I felt that I had been too lucky. I slid the lower sash of the window softly upward and stepped into the room. I could see the bookcase clearly in the moonlight, and put my hand at hazard behind a row of handsomely bound volumes on the middle shelf. My hand came down on a soft chamois leather bag. I could feel the diamonds in it. I was absolutely certain that I had got them, and as certain that I should not keep them. This last stroke of luck frightened me.

As I withdrew my hand with the chamois bag in it it struck against a little knob that slid back easily, and immediately the bookcase began to move. I guessed what had happened. The bookcase screened an entrance into another room, and moved easily, though very slowly, by some mechanical device; I had inadvertently struck my hand against the knob which set the machinery in motion. Almost immediately I saw a thin streak of light running half-way up the wall and gradually widening. The next room was therefore lit up. I felt in my waistcoat pocket to see if that special cigarette to be used in cases of desperation was still in its proper place, and then stood back in the shadow and awaited events. The bookcase moved back until it disclosed a full-sized doorway, but with no door in it, and through this the light streamed into the room where I was standing. And with the light there came a strong scent of lilies and gardenias, heavy and oppressive.

All this had happened in absolute silence, except for the slight grunting of the machinery as the bookcase moved. I stood and waited, counting very slowly in my head. I counted up to five hundred, and still there was no sound of movement from the next room. The silence indeed seemed to be more intense than ever. I stepped out of my corner into the lighted doorway.

This room was a bedroom. On a small, and I should say cheap, iron bedstead in the middle of the room lay the dead body of Sir Charles. I will not describe him; a fat man does not look pretty when he is dead. The half-closed eyes seemed to be looking straight at me. The windows were heavily curtained, and on the bed itself and on the floor were masses of white flowers; the electric light was full on, and, in addition, a row of tall candles blazed at the head of the bed. I drew the chamois leather bag from my pocket and emptied out the diamonds into the palm of my hand. They were few in number, but magnificent in size and quality. I should say that the Colonel had decidedly underestimated them when he put their value at five thousand pounds.

I put the diamonds back in the bag, advanced towards the body and put the bag with the diamonds in it in the horrible pasty hand of the dead man. Then I went out.

With the living it is another affair, but the dead man wins, so far as I am concerned. I would not that night have taken one farthing from him for any consideration. I found my way back safely to the field, and wandered about for hours until the dawn came. A little later I got an early train on to Guildford, but I did not take the motor-car back to London at once. I went to the principal hotel and ordered a bedroom. I needed rest. And it had also become necessary for me to get intoxicated.

II

RECLAMATION WORK

At one time wives and families of men who were serving their sentences in prison frequently suffered great privation. In sheer desperation they would often be themselves driven to dishonest courses to procure the bare means of existence, and in this way the punishment of crime was in reality the cause of its multiplication. To a lesser extent this evil still prevails, though I should be doing less than justice did I not mention the splendid efforts of several organisations, and notably of the Church Army, to deal with it. I sometimes did what I could in this direction myself.

When Alfred Gimbrell, a criminal of feeble type and low intelligence, got what he termed a tray of moons, he had a message conveyed to me that he would take it very kind if I would keep an eye on the missus and the kids. He had a large family, and was an affectionate husband and father. I provided them with a small sum of money for their immediate necessities, and set about finding work for the woman. In this I had no difficulty. It was in the height of the London season, and many firms were giving temporary employment to extra hands. Moreover, Mrs Gimbrell was a really clever woman with her needle. I told the plain facts of the case to Messrs Pawling & Ramsworthy of Oxford Street, and they agreed to take her on if I would guarantee the value of the materials entrusted to her. To this I at once consented; I have done the same thing in several cases, and I have never lost a penny by it. Five of the children were at school, the eldest girl helped her mother, and the eldest boy sold newspapers. From time to time, when I was in the neighbourhood, I looked in to see how they were getting on. To my mind they seemed to be doing better without Alfred than with him.

Mrs Gimbrell was touchingly grateful.

"If ever Alf goes crooked again," she said, "after all you've done, Mr Dix, he ought to be took out and shot, though it's his own wife that says it."

"Ah, Mrs Gimbrell," I said, "why did you not use your influence to check him before he got into this trouble? Time after time you must have known that the money he brought in was not made honestly. "

"Well, what was I to do? After all, it's for 'im to look after me; it's not for me to look after 'im. It's not for a married woman to set and slave while the man spends the money. He ain't bad many ways. He don't drink—leastways not like some. And fond of 'is children? O not 'arf! Why, he'd cut 'is 'and off at the root for 'em. But then it seems like as if he couldn't work. He's one of them that gets soon tired—that's where it is, and the money 'ad got to come from somewhere."

"And now you see where it leads to."

"Yes, we'll 'ave a change now. That I'm determined on. If you could only speak to him! He's out Saturday morning, and then it's just the few weeks before we all goes down to the hop-picking. That always suits him—looks a better man every time when he comes back If he'd keep straight for them few weeks there might be a chance."

"I will do what I can. On Sunday afternoon I shall be giving a short address in Hyde Park. Bring him to hear me and I will see that what I say is specially suited to his case. Yes, I know that it's a long way, but the walk will do you both good. And when the address is over I will have a few words with him privately."

She thanked me again and I left.

I had been on the verge of telling her to send him up to my house in Lanyon Street, Bloomsbury, on Saturday night But I remembered that Saturday would be the first of August, and I had already arranged for my evening on the first of August.

I proceed with some regret to tell what my arrangements were. I know very well that if these memoirs are ever published, I shall be then far beyond the reach of men's contempt. But I seem already to feel the sting of that word Hypocrite, though it has never at this moment of writing been applied to me. The finest temperance sermon I ever heard was preached by a clergyman who was, as was discovered subsequently, himself a dipsomaniac. I knew the man, and he was no hypocrite. I am as convinced of my ability to reclaim others as of the utter hopelessness of any attempt to reclaim myself. I am a good preacher, but I am a very good thief. Theft happens to be the thing that I do best. I have studied it, and I am fond of it. It gives me a great satisfaction to note the blunders that lead less intelligent criminals to their destruction, and the way in which I avoid those blunders. Again, though I have a house at a fairly high rental in Bloomsbury, and a smaller house at Brighton, and paid close on five hundred pounds for my motor-car, and live very comfortably, a certain portion of my income is set aside for my work among the criminals and the suffering of the East End of London.

On the first of July—one month before—I happened to be in the bank in the afternoon, and after finishing my business I was chatting about the political situation with the cashier, to whom I am well known. I am well known as a philanthropist to quite a number of respectable people. The manager of Messrs Pawling & Ramsworthy always has a tolerant smile for me when I tell him of any of my cases, and will help me if he can do so without risk to himself. I am sure the last time that Ikey got into trouble Inspector Measor was almost apologetic about it, though at the same time he told me that he was afraid I should find Ikey a hopeless case. I am known as a thief to myself alone. As the cashier was talking, a little old woman stepped up to the counter and I stood aside for her. She was dressed very neatly in a by-gone fashion, and gave one the idea of a particular and prim person. As soon as the cashier saw her he produced a canvas bag, and as she handed in her cheque, pushed the bag across to her.

"Thank you, sir. I wish you good afternoon," she said. She put the money in a locked leather bag she was carrying, and went out. I saw the cheque upside-down for the fraction of a second, as the cashier took it to his desk (out of sight) to obliterate the signature. It was a cheque for fifty pounds, payable to order, but the word 'bearer' had been substituted and initiated. It was signed Hannah Gosforth in a small and particularly neat hand-writing.

"You had it all ready for her," I said. "How did you know what she wanted?"

"It's the same on the first of every month—or the second if the first happens to be a Sunday. Has banked here for the last thirty years, though she lives at Surbiton; and unless she's ill or away on a holiday she always comes herself for it. Never counts it either—says that if she thought I were dishonest or couldn't count, she'd bank somewhere else. Queer customer."

There is a type of woman that always gets an order cheque-book for safety, and always alters "order" to "bearer" for convenience. She carries fifty pounds in gold through a crowded thoroughfare in a silly hand-bag at the time when a man of observation might be expecting her, and thinks herself secure because the bag has a penny-farthing lock on it. I know that type. I know the kind of cash-box which it uses and trusts. I know its reading-lamp, its lavender sachets, and its bright keys, and its religious observances. There was a time (back in my boyhood) when I knew some of its charm; and I know now all its futility.

Fifty pounds is not a large sum perhaps to a rich man. But I felt that it would be worth my while to take it, especially as the trouble attending it promised to be very slight. I could not go to Surbiton that day, as I had promised to attend a meeting in Clerkenwell in the evening; besides I should have an equally good opportunity in a month's time. I was anxious to make my visit on the first of the month, because it struck me that a woman who always drew fifty on the first, would be extremely likely to pay the house-books of the previous month on the second, and her domestic servants on the third.

The first of August was a Saturday, and therefore the second was a Sunday—a day on which I felt assured that Miss Hannah Gosforth would neither make nor receive payments. Why then did I not postpone my visit to the Sunday? Simply because I happen to share Miss Gosforth's views as to the observance of Sunday. I give up the whole of Sunday to what I think to be the higher branch of my work, and frequently I have given as many as six addresses in the one day. I should not dream of making money on Sunday. And I have a conviction—the infidel will call it stupid fatalism—that if I ever break my rule the last calamity will follow.

So on a Saturday afternoon I put a packet of sandwiches in one side-pocket of the jacket of a blue serge suit, and a flask of cold weak tea, flavoured with lemon, in the other side-pocket. I have no objection to drinking intoxicating liquors when I wish to become intoxicated, as from time to time occurs, but for ordinary drinking I have found cold tea to be the most useful. It should be very weak—strong tea affects the nerves, and my nerves are important—and the flavour of lemon blends pleasantly. In the breast-pocket of the same jacket I carried a letter to Miss Hannah Gosforth. Inside was the circular of a new and pushing boot-making company which had been left in my own letter-box that morning. On the envelope was a particularly illegible address, written by myself. I have no false modesty about it. In these memoirs I state facts only, and you can draw your own conclusions. It is a fact that I am a master in the art of writing partially illegible addresses. You could just make out the name of Miss Gosforth, and you could decipher the word "street." The word Surbition was written in a larger hand and was clear enough for anybody. But the number and name of the street were quite illegible. With this I had very little doubt that I should be able to discover Miss Gosforth's place of residence. When I arrived at Surbiton I went into the first shop of any importance that I came across and showed the letter. "A friend," I said, "asked me to deliver this while I was in Surbiton, and I can't make head or tail of the address. It's for a Miss Gosforth. I wonder if you could help me?"

The man to whom I was speaking had approached with the usual obsequious smile. He now looked distinctly sulky.

"No," he said, "I can't help you. Miss Gosforth don't deal here."

It was clear to me that Miss Gosforth had at one time dealt there, and had subsequently transferred her custom; also that the man knew her address perfectly well and had not the remotest intention of giving it; so I thanked him and went out. I then tried a postman with the same story.

"Yes," he said, "I know Miss Hannah Gosforth well enough, but that address is wrong. It's not a street, it's a road—Marley Road. Ivy Cottage, Marley Road, that's where she lives, and it's pretty well the last house."

I gave the man a shilling, and a few minutes later was ringing the bell at Ivy Cottage. I handed my letter to the servant and went off. I had thus made my observations of the place under circumstances unlikely to cause suspicion.

Ivy Cottage was a small detached house with a scrap of garden between it and the road, and a larger garden behind. I had seen through the window the old lady's methodical writing-table. It was of the kind known as an Oxford table, and I had very little doubt that she kept her useless cash box in one of the bottom drawers of that table, locked it with an equally useless key, and slept with a conviction that she had done all that a mortal woman could do to defend her property, and might leave the rest to Providence. Any of the windows on the ground floor could be opened with ease, but to prevent observation from the road I decided to take one of the windows at the back.

I wandered away into the country, finished my sandwiches and tea, and made notes for my addresses on the following day. It was a beautifully warm and peaceful evening, with that strange calm in it that I have often noticed in the country on the eve of Sunday, as though Nature like man, now prepared for a while to rest

I was back at Ivy Cottage by half-past ten. By that time I felt certain that the old lady and her household would be in bed and asleep, and I knew that I could do what I had to do quietly and very quickly.

In the garden behind the house I found a man standing with his back to me, spreading with some care a sheet of brown paper with treacle.

I do not mean that under the doubtful light of the stars I could detect that the paper was brown, or that it was treacle that was being used. That was a matter of conjecture. But I saw enough to be sure that here was a man on the point of effecting a burglarious entrance into Miss Gosforth's house. The treacle-spread sheet of stiff paper is applied to a pane of the window, and the glass can then generally be broken and removed without noise. The broken pieces adhere to the paper. The man gets his arm through the hole, feels for any electric alarm wires and cuts them, and then puts back the catch and opens the window. I have used this old trick myself, but I seldom employ it now. The treacle must be of just the right consistency, and the whole thing must be managed with great skill, or the trick fails and a noise is made which awakes the people in the house. It is not certain enough for me.

Intentionally, I took a step on the gravel. It was enough. The man turned sharply, saw, me, and then dropped his bottle and the paper, and made a bolt for the road. I ran after him.

Twenty yards down the road I had almost overhauled my man, when he turned sharp round and his hand went to his side-pocket

"Stop that, Alfred Gimbrell," I said. "Do you want to kill the man who saved your wife and children?"

He had not recognised me, though I had never had any doubt about him. He used the extremely filthy and blasphemous expression which was habitual with him when he wished to indicate great surprise and astonishment, and then he pulled out his revolver and handed it to me.

"There yer are," he said. "Put my lights out. I deserve it."

"You are talking foolishly, Gimbrell," I said. "I shall take this weapon because you are not to be trusted with it. But it was not to kill you that I came to Surbiton tonight. It was to save you from the consequences of your own folly and wickedness."

"I suppose, Mr Dix, it's no good astin' you how you knew I was on this lay?"

I answered him with another question. "Where did you buy this revolver?" I had noticed that it was new and had not been used.

He thought it over for a moment. "I see," he said. "And so you followed me on from there. Why, you'd make a 'tec'. I never knew you was near me. O blast it! What's the good?"

"Don't swear, Gimbrell. Bad language, as I have told you before, is something worse than useless. Come along quietly with me and tell me how you come to be doing this when you have only been for a few hours out of prison?"

We walked away from the town and he talked as we went.

"If you arst me how I knew of it, I had it from a friend, who got it from a pal of his that knows the servant. My friend was to have took half what I got."

"Ah, Gimbrell, that was no true friend."

"And so I told him myself. Two quid I wouldn't have stuck at. But what right had he got to half, with me taking all the risks?"

"No true friend would have tempted you back to your old way of life at all; I tell you, Gimbrell, you'll have to quit it."

"That's what I was wanting to do. But yer see how it was. I come 'ome and finds the missus very 'aughty and teachin' of my own kids to look on me as if I was a leper. I know she had some money, but there wasn't so much as the price of a pot for me. I could go out and see if I couldn't find a job of work, she said. Nice words those are to use to any man! Then I come on my friend and he got talking. You see, you must have a bit of something in your pocket to be going on with while you're looking for some suitable occupation. This was to have been the last time. And it was a soft thing—fifty golden sovereigns and all as easy as telling lies. Mind you I wasn't going to be took again. I'd have outed the copper and myself too. I wouldn't go till my friend gave me the money to get this revolver. And that's the kind of man as my missus turns on and says, 'O cawn't you go and get yerself a job of work?' Just like that! And I assure you, Mr Dix, that's a woman I've never so much as raised my 'and against. What I warnt to know is if I'm expected to stand such treatment as that, while—"

"Never mind that. Your wife has worked hard and well to keep the home together while you were in prison. You should try to win back her respect."

"She'd have respected me fast enough if I'd come 'ome tonight with them quids in my pocket."

"There you are mistaken. While you have been away she has learned to look at things very differently."

"So she told me—going on as if I wasn't good enough for her."

His wife had evidently been very tactless. In many ways I felt sorry for the man. I determined to see if I could not break through his miserable conceit and his utter recklessness, and touch his heart. With the utmost fervour and sincerity I threw myself into the work I spoke to him of his children. I said much which need not be repeated here. And in the end I succeeded. I had the man weeping and penitent, and I had his most solemn promise that he would lead a new life in the future. Then I gave him a few shillings to pay his fare back and get himself some supper, and sent him off.

In Gimbrell's flight from the house and my pursuit of him a certain amount of noise must have been made. It would not have surprised me if I had found the house lit up. But it was all in darkness, and not a sound was to be heard. I went round to the back and found the sheet of brown paper and the bottle that Gimbrell had dropped. I had not intended to use anything of the kind, but as it was there and all ready prepared I fitted the sheet to a pane of glass. It worked very well.

I met with no incidents of interest while I was in the house. I was there for only a few moments. The cash-box was not in the drawers of the table, but in a little locked cupboard in the sideboard. It was much as I expected. It had a triple lock, and looked very substantial. The bottom of it was a separate piece fastened in with four screws. It was made in Germany, and if these lines should ever come to the eye of its maker, I hope that he will let me take this opportunity of saying that I am obliged to him. It contained £40, 6S. 3d. It was less than I had expected. But I think I made up the difference with a pair of saltcellars, genuine Queen Anne, and very interesting. I intended these for my own use. I left Gimbrell's revolver behind me. I never carry anything of that kind. The police were very pleased at finding it, but they did not succeed in tracing the purchaser of it.

Gimbrell, who heard of the old lady's loss, was much impressed with the coincidences that the case presented. "Why," he said, "If I'd only gone a bit later, and you hadn't been following me, that other bloke and me might have met in the 'ouse. It would 'ave made me angry, but I couldn't have helped laughing."

III

WITH A CLEAR CONSCIENCE

I have already disclaimed any overmastering ambitions. I care nothing about the *coup* for its own sake. There are men who seek out the difficult *coup* just as an artist may intentionally seek difficulties of subject or treatment in a story or picture. I prefer easy work, when I can get it. Nor has wealth any such charms for me that I would take absurd risks to obtain it. For years past an annual income of £2000 has satisfied me. I live regularly, and am aware that any sudden increase of means and expenditure with nothing to account for it, is likely to render one an object of suspicion. All thieves know this, but comparatively few can bring themselves to act upon it.

Take, for instance, the case of Ikey. He is not unintelligent. As an Inspector of an Electric Lighting Company he is admirable. He carries a note-book with the right name and address of the Company stamped in gold on its morocco cover, and the book is partly filled with notes and figures that would deceive anybody except an electrician. He carries a printed card of authorisation and a little brown bag with apparatus in it. The apparatus consists of a compass, a screwdriver, and two coils of bell-wire, so it is not remarkably electrical. But it suffices; in fact Ikey has said to me that no servant in London is able to doubt him after he has once opened that bag and produced the bell-wire. He knows nothing whatever of electricity. He told one old lady in Berkeley Square that the *ampere* wanted cleaning, and he was afraid he would have to unscrew the volts. But he knows when it is best for him to look very serious and to say very little. In this way he has in one morning cleared a thousand pound's worth of diamonds from a good house in the West End. Naturally the "fence" gave him rather less than one-tenth of this sum, but it was too much for Ikey. He could not resist new clothes, some showy jewellery, and an inclination to stand drinks freely, and to brag of his *coup*. So, of course, the police got him.

There are times when I have undertaken an adventure of considerable risk for the sake of a considerable profit. There was, for instance, the case of the Manton-on-Sea branch of Appleby, Hanson & Lane's Bank. I had just purchased my motor-car, one of my three banking accounts were very low, and I did not wish to realise investments. The risks were great, but they were not absurd; the branch was in temporary premises at the time, and one or two accidental circumstances were in my favour. It was merely necessary for me to drug three people, and I did it. The manager himself was a teetotaller, and as earnest and God-fearing a man as ever I saw; but he was a bit of a hypochondriac and quite ready to try my new medicine. I felt sorry for him at the time. The amount of gold was much less than I had expected, and I did not care to touch the notes, but on the whole I was fairly satisfied. Still I avoid such work as a rule. The only way by which I care to open a good safe or strong room is by its own proper keys, and too many accidents are possible in getting and using them.

That business with the Bank then turned out more easy than I had expected. Frequently the reverse has been the case. I have taken on something that looked perfectly soft and simple, and have given weeks of time and thought before I could bring it to a successful issue. This was the case with the miser of

Darwen village. I was stopping at Brighton at the time, and in the course of a long walk I stopped for rest and refreshment at the Crown Inn at Darwen. It is a quiet and old-fashioned inn, with a comfortable and sleepy landlord. As I sat chatting with my host a little old man came in of strange appearance. He was very dirty and very ragged. He had a timid and watery eye, and thin lips pressed tightly together. His rags were not those that would have been worn by a labourer, nor was his appearance that of one of the labouring class. His voice, as I noticed when he spoke, was that of a man of refinement and education.

"Good morning, Mr Jacobs," said the landlord, with something like a wink in my direction, as though to bid me watch what would happen.

"Good morning, sir," said the old man. "A beautiful morning for walking, though the air is somewhat chilly. I have called in because I have a present to make you. I wish to give you something."

The landlord grinned good-humouredly. The little old man dived into the pocket of his shabby grey overcoat and pulled out two large apples.

"There, sir," he said, "I should not say it, but they are beautiful fruit. You will find nothing like them in Darwen. And I will trouble you for sixpennyworth of brandy."

The landlord, still grinning, put the apples on a shelf and measured out the old man's drink. Mr Jacobs had with the apples pulled out an empty clay pipe, gazed at it, and then up at the ceiling.

"There is some delicious tobacco being smoked in this room," he said reflectively. "I like to drink in its fragrance for a minute or two before I spoil it with my pipeful of a ranker and cheaper variety. The poor must not expect too much. I have always maintained that the poor are wrong when they expect too much."

I was the only man in the room who was smoking and I passed my pouch over to him.

"Thank you, sir," he said, "I did not intend to trespass upon you in this way—nothing was further from my thoughts. Still, as you so kindly insist, I will partake."

He filled his clay pipe and palmed some more of the tobacco, when he thought that he was unobserved. He lit his pipe with a match from the stand, and in an absent-minded way slid a few of the matches into his pocket. Then he turned to the landlord. "And how much am I indebted to you, sir, for this refreshment?"

"Why, nothing, Mr Jacobs. Surely, if I accept your presents, I may offer you a friendly glass."

"If you wish it, let it be so. You are very kind. The world is in many respects better than the cynics would have us believe. There are still great and generous hearts. Good morning to both of you."

He went out, and the landlord immediately burst out laughing.

"That's a queer old chap," I said.

"He is," said the landlord. "They call him the miser of Darwen. He is worth twenty-five thousand pounds, so they say, and he lives alone in a cottage that isn't fit to keep a dog in. I have never seen a penny of his money in my life. He brings fruit or he brings vegetables, and goes through the same bit of playacting that you saw just now. Of course I don't want his apples; everybody has got more apples than they can give away this year. It's the same with all his presents, but I don't care. The old chap always makes me laugh, and it's dull enough in a little place like this. Besides he can't last much longer, and who knows but what he may remember me? He tried the same game on at the Blue Boar, bottom of the village, but the chap there wouldn't have it. Did you twig him sneaking your baccy?"

This was interesting. I got the landlord to tell me all he knew about Jacobs. He was, it appeared, in receipt of an annuity of two pounds per week, and for the last thirty years, so the villagers computed, he had never spent more than six shillings a week. His garden and cottage were his own freehold; the cottage was in a most wretched condition, but he refused to spend a penny on it. Once a year (the villagers said it was on his birthday) he would give a child a penny to whiten the step in front of his door, and for weeks afterwards would avoid using that step. But with this exception he did everything for himself. Sometimes he even earned a little money; he was, the landlord said, a scholar, and had written letters for people in the village in cases where a noble and correct style was felt to be worth a penny a page. He had no bank account, and it was supposed that his savings were hidden in his cottage, which he would never leave for more than a quarter of an hour at a time. "Not that he need trouble himself," said the landlord, "for we are all honest in Darwen. Like to see the old chap's shanty? It's only just across the road there."

All of this seemed to me to be particularly good. There would be no twenty-five thousand, of course, but there would be a sum very well worth taking, and, so it seemed at the time, very easy to take. I told the landlord that I should stop at his inn for a day or two. I did not think so simple a business could possibly take longer. In reality I stopped there a month, and was compelled to neglect my reformation work in London in a way I greatly regretted. However, I went back there at the end of that month with renewed health and strength from my holiday in the country—and with something else besides.

The next time I encountered Jacobs was again in the bar of the Crown. He had presented with great solemnity three exceedingly small potatoes, and had ordered a pint of old ale very much as if he had an intention of paying for it. It was easy enough to get into conversation with him; he himself began it.

"I cannot but remember you, sir. That one little pipe of your excellent tobacco has been fragrant in my memory ever since."

I renewed his acquaintance with it, and asked him if he could tell me of any one in the village who would call in the evening to take my letters to the post, and could do neat and legible copying.

"Might I enquire what the terms would be?"

I satisfied him on this point, and he turned the matter over in his own mind. The post office was a full mile from his own cottage, but the copying work which I had added by way of bait attracted him. "I am, sir," he said, "a Bachelor of Arts of the University of Oxford. I admit that I do not look it, but it is the case. I shall be pleased to undertake the copying on the terms you suggest, and any passer-by will always be willing to post your letters for you."

I explained to him that this would not do; it was essential that my letters should be posted by a responsible person—someone whom I could trust, not a chance person who might lose them or forget them or stay to talk on the way and thus miss the post. Finally, though with some apparent misgiving, he gave way.

The lock of the cottage door presented no difficulties. I went all over the place that night while Jacobs was away at the post. It was a three-roomed cottage, standing in a small garden with a few fruit trees at the back. It looked disreputable enough on the outside. The roof was crazy and half covered with ivy. Windows were patched and gutters broken. Clouds of flies hovered over the fœtid green water in the butt at the corner of the house. On the other hand, the garden was well-kept and cultivated. There were no flowers there; the miser grew nothing that he could not eat. And the interior of the cottage surprised me. It was more tidy and cleaner than I had expected. What little furniture there was seemed for the most part to have been made by the miser himself from old packing-cases. There were hanging bookshelves on the walls, and the books in them were all classical. In fact I found the "Phaedo" lying open on the kitchen table. But I did not find any trace of the hidden treasure. After three more visits I came to the conclusion that it could not be in the cottage at all. I had probed and examined everywhere, and it could not have escaped me. So I gave up the cottage and tried the garden. It seemed to me quite likely that the old man buried his money; his gardening operations would provide a useful cover for it.

I learned that garden by heart. I knew every inch of it, and day after day I waited to see if there were any disturbance of the soil that might give me a clue. Hidden by the high hedge at the further end I watched the old man at work there. I tried the trunks of the fruit trees, to see if they could be used as a hiding-place. All was in vain. The miser's gardening was of the most ordinary and genuine description, and his trees were all solid. I had gone into this matter as if it were child's play, and it was giving me far more trouble than the Bank's local branch had done. I took to watching the place at night, and all that I could discover was that the old man slept from nine to five with the utmost regularity. I began to think that the money could not be there at all. But I had assured myself of the existence of the annuity, and that Jacobs did not spend the money, and that he did not bank it. Where then could it be?

I might have remained in ignorance to this day if it had not been for the fact that one afternoon a sandy-coloured gutter-cat went to sleep on the path just outside the miser's garden gate. She awoke as a group of boys came along from school, and slipped through into the garden. The foremost boy sent a stone after her and missed her. The stone struck the water-butt. I had witnessed the little incident, and I now knew where Jacobs kept his savings. The sound the stone made was not what it would have been if the butt had been full of water—as it apparently was, and as I had always supposed it to be.

I went back to the inn, had a cup of tea, and wrote a reply to a letter I had received from my friend the Reverend Arthur Hope, asking when he could see me in town about a poor family in which we were both interested. I was able to give him an appointment for two days later.

That night I sent Jacobs off with my letter to the post, and made an examination. The butt consisted of a large barrel standing on end, and divided just above the bung-hole into two parts. The upper part was filled with water. The money was kept in the lower part. The bung was easily removed, but I could not get my hand in. With my stick I could feel down on to a concrete floor heaped with coins.

I was in no hurry now. I went back to my rooms and thought the thing over. The old fool had used this place with success for years, and had probably grown very confident about it. He dropped his sovereigns through the bung-hole, and loved to think how they were accumulating. It was the only pleasure money could give him. Every miser is a madman. If I had taken the hoard that night it is quite possible that he would never have discovered his loss. But if he did, it was also quite likely that suspicion would fall on me. To divert it I should have had to remain in the place for some time longer and to have continued the farce of giving him employment. This would have been very tiresome to me. So I left for London the following morning without the money.

About six weeks later I was stopping at my Brighton house, and I thought that I might as well walk over to Darwen one night. I chose a dark night, and took precautions to establish an *alibi* if one should prove necessary. At the time that I was walking to Darwen my household was convinced that I was asleep in bed.

I had at first intended to cut a hole through the barrel and get the money that way. But I gave up this idea; it would have made it quite certain that the miser would find out his loss.

The method I chose was to fish for the money. It was the more tedious way, but it would leave no immediate evidence that the hoard had been disturbed; and if nothing were found out it might be worth my while to try the same thing again in a year or two. I do not know why, but I was very nervous about this simple affair—possibly because it had given me so much trouble at the outset. For instance, I had provided myself with a loaded line and a tin of bird-lime, but I decided that these things came within the category of suspicious apparatus. I took with me instead a bottle of my hairdresser's "Moustacheoline." This is an innocent preparation for fixing the moustache. It is a fluid, but on exposure to the air it becomes hard and intensely sticky.

Half a mile outside Darwen I left the road and took to the fields. I approached Jacobs' cottage from the back. The whole place was as still as a little village generally is at midnight. I had cut a little sprig of furze and tied it to the end of a string. I smeared this with the preparation, and attached to it the seal I wore on my watch-chain to serve as a weight. Then I knelt beside the water-butt and lowered my line through the bunghole. The first time I got four sovereigns, and the second time three. Once or twice a coin fell back on the heap just as I was raising it, and I would wait a minute or two until I was sure that the chink had not by any chance been heard. It was a slow and laborious business, and all the time I was most unaccountably timid and jumpy. When I had got two hundred and fifty I gave up, though I was nothing like at the end of the heap. I got back home without any adventure of any kind, but when I met a policeman in Brighton streets I nearly jumped out of my skin, and though I was dead tired when I got home I was too excited to sleep. I was thoroughly ashamed of myself, and if my nerves often gave way like this I should at once choose some other means of providing for myself. I believe in proper precautions, and I despise the recklessness which sooner or later is sure to end in detection. But when once the plan is made and the decision taken there should be calm presence of mind in its execution, and this I had not shown. I record my weakness, because in these pages I wish to give the truth without self-glorification.

A week later, finding that Jacobs had never apparently discovered his loss, I walked into Darwen and had a talk with him. He was just going into the Crown, and had a small cauliflower with him. He seemed a little hurt that the landlord did not show more enthusiasm about that cauliflower, but otherwise he was quite happy. I felt that I had done a good action. He was none the worse, and I was two hundred and fifty pounds the better. Money was meant to be used.

In the course of the next year I paid two other nocturnal visits to Mr Jacob's water-butt. On the first occasion, when I was interrupted, I took thirty pounds, and on the next when I was able to give more time to it I secured three hundred and eighty. On both of these occasions I was pleased to find that my nerves were in their normal condition. With this I was satisfied, though I might have gone back again but for the poor old man's sudden death from double pneumonia. In his will he left a statement of the sum that would be found in the bottom of the water-butt; and this was discovered by his executors to be quite inaccurate. There was a shortage of six hundred and sixty pounds, a sum for which they will if they ever read my memoirs now be able to account. As it was, they decided that the old man must have hidden this money elsewhere and forgotten all about it. They searched the house and the garden with the utmost thoroughness; the whole of the garden was dug up and the cottage was nearly pulled down. And even then, when the property came into the market it fetched twice its proper value as the purchaser believed that he had a chance of finding the missing six hundred and sixty.

Jacob's executors were his solicitors, and after their expenses had been paid the rest of his money went to his old college, St Cecilia's, at Oxford. His college had refused him the Fellowship which he had confidently expected, and since that time he had had no connection with it. There was no reason why he should have left his money there, and I was glad that I had been able to rescue six hundred and sixty of it from aiding an institution for providing a classical and useless education. Not one penny was left to the landlord of the Crown who had frequently and in many ways befriended the old miser.

I am not accustomed to feel remorse for any theft that I may commit. I am a born thief, and I thieve very well; theft is a thing, as I have said, that I do best and like best. But it is seldom that I can look back on any of my operations with the immense satisfaction that this has given me. Jacobs was not a man who, in a really civilised country, would have been allowed to possess any money at all, and my only regret is that I did not take more.

IV

CHECKMATE

I think I have already mentioned that Mr Stanwick, the managing director of Messrs Pawling & Ramsworthy, was a friend of mine, and occasionally helped me to find work for some of those whose reclamation I was attempting. It therefore was with great regret that I stole his valuable collection of stamps in which, as I was aware, he took an immense interest. The circumstances which made this action on my part necessary may be given briefly, and will explain exactly how it happened.

Mrs Gimbrell, the wife of a criminal of low intelligence, had, as I have told previously, been given work by Pawling & Ramsworthy. I guaranteed the cost of materials entrusted to her. She had a cousin, Mrs Sanders, a widow, who, in the rare intervals of her intoxication had seemed to me to show abilities of a rather unusual order. She could draw and design fairly well. Naturally her bad habits prevented her from getting regular work and kept her in a condition of the most miserable poverty. Mrs Gimbrell had a very proper desire to persuade her cousin to lead a new life, and consulted me on the subject.

"Fust, she drinks because she ain't got nothing else to do, and then she ain't got nothing else to do because she drinks. And that's how it is. Goes on and on like. But she's a woman as might make a good living twenty different ways. So far as cleverness of the head goes I don't know that I wouldn't put her before myself."

"And what," I asked, "do you think we could do?"

"Well, it's this wye. If I were to come to her with work in my hand and say, 'Now then, Gladys, you take and do this and you'll be well paid for it, and there's plenty more where that came from so long as you keep sober,' then that'd be talking."

I promised her that I would do what I could, and I took some specimens of her drawings to show to my friend Mr Stanwick. As it happened his firm was making at that time rather a speciality of water-colour drawings of dresses. Customers could look through the portfolio and find the kind of thing that they wanted. The firm found this a very satisfactory way of dealing with some of their best exclusive ideas. A model in a window or showroom is easily seen, remembered, and copied by a clever dressmaker. The portfolio was only shown to customers with whom the firm was acquainted. He agreed to give Gladys Sanders a trial, and I guaranteed the firm against any loss due to her for a space of one month. During that month she did admirably, showed great resource, and produced several novelties out of which the firm made a good profit. They kept her on, but they did not renew the guarantee. This may have been carelessness—Stanwick himself said it was an oversight—but I think myself that they had been convinced too readily of the woman's honesty and ability and did not think the guarantee necessary. She was well paid, had no one but herself to support, and was now infinitely better off than her cousin, Mrs Gimbrell, who had befriended her. There was no excuse whatever for what she did. I am sorry to say that she took sketches of the whole of Messrs Pawling & Ramsworthy's Spring novelties and sold them to an unscrupulous opposition establishment. Naturally Stanwick was furious and sent for me. I offered there and then to make good the money loss, so far as it could be calculated, that the firm had incurred, although I was not legally bound to do anything of the kind. Stanwick would not hear of it. He said he did not want my money. He simply stamped up and down the room saying that it was the last time he would do anything for my damned East-Enders, and that he would employ respectable people in future. He expressed delight that Mrs Sanders was in prison, and hoped that she would drink herself to hell as soon as she came out. I begged him to moderate his language; but it is of little use to argue with an angry man. Out of sheer spite and vindictiveness he stopped giving out any further work to Mrs Gimbrell, though the firm had always found her honest and skilful, and were in her case fully protected by my guarantee.

The work was not essential to Mrs Gimbrell. Alfred had now got a post as night-watchman, and the family could have lived on what he made. But undoubtedly the money that Mrs Gimbrell earned was very useful to them. They had, it will be remembered, a large family. I waited for a week to give Stanwick's temper time to cool down, and then I called on him again with reference to Mrs Gimbrell. He was good enough to say that he was always pleased to see me whenever I looked in to have a chat with him, but on the other point he was as obstinate as ever. I saw that if I pressed the subject it would only end in his losing his temper again. So I left with a sad heart that such cruelty and obstinacy should be possible in the world, and with the decision to steal Mr Stanwick's collection of postage stamps. Those who will not lend a hand in the work of reclamation, and try to thrust back a poor woman like Mrs Gimbrell struggling out of the mire, should be punished in a way that they will feel. I was sure that Stanwick would feel the loss of his collection acutely.

Mr Stanwick lived in a handsome, but rather pretentious house on Wimbledon Common. I had frequently dined there and knew the place well. The stamp collection was kept in the library in an unlocked bookcase. It had been begun by his father, and was now being completed by himself. I have known several cases of hereditary philately. He had told me some years before that he would not take fifteen hundred pounds for the collection, and as he was adding to it from time to time I supposed that it would be worth more now. The system of bolts, locks and burglar alarms in his house was really ingenious. There was hardly a window in the place which could have been easily and safely opened at night by a burglar with a common pocket-knife. There are very few houses of which one can say as much as that. And Stanwick himself always tested the alarms before going to bed.

I did not propose therefore to force my admission into Stanwick's house. I always try the easiest way first. There is a convict at present in Portland who spent five hours and a half on one safe, and then discovered that the thing was not locked at all. I selected a night when Stanwick was giving a big dinner-party. At the moment when everybody was most busy I opened the back door, stepped across a passage to the coal-cellar, entered it, shut the door and sat down. Nothing could have been simpler. My only objection was that the waiting was rather tiresome. I had no light, and therefore could not read or write. To occupy my mind I thought out the address which I was to deliver on the following Sunday. I heard the last carriage drive away and Stanwick's tired servants going up to bed, but it was not till an hour after that, that Stanwick made his rounds. He is really a singularly thorough and careful man. I heard him locking doors, sliding bolts, and testing electric alarms. At last he went up to bed. Ten minutes later I was walking along the road in the direction of Putney with Stanwick's stamp collection under my arm. A policeman told me that I had missed the last 'bus, but I was lucky enough to find a belated hansom. I went to sleep, well satisfied with my night's work. Stanwick had no right to punish Mrs Gimbrell for the faults of Mrs Sanders. It was an act of abominable injustice that made my blood boil.

This, by the way, is the only time in my life that I have taken anything that I did not want. I have not the faintest interest in stamps, and I did not propose to take the bother or run the risk of disposing of the collection.

Three days later I called on Stanwick at his place of business in Oxford Street. He seemed to be in the best of spirits, and chaffed me about my usual refusal to have a whisky-and-soda.

"You seem very cheerful, Stanwick," I said. "Anything happened to you?"

"Yes," he said, "something has happened to me. I have had a bit of luck."

"I am very glad to hear it," I said. "Somebody been leaving you money?"

"No, I have had a burglary at my house."

"You don't say so!"

"Fact last Wednesday night somebody or other managed to get into my house. How it was done I cannot imagine. The wire of the burglar alarm was cut against one of the library windows, but how the man managed to get in to cut it I can't conceive. The police think he must have been concealed on the premises, but that doesn't seem to me to be likely. Somebody or other would have been certain to have seen him."

It was by the window of the library that I had made my exit after first cutting the wire.

"I see," I said. "So that's your bit of luck? The chap got scared, and left before he had time to take anything."

"Not a bit of it. That's the queer part of it I'm in luck because the burglar did take something. He took my collection of stamps."

"I confess that I don't see it. I thought you valued that collection particularly."

"So I did, and it's because I did that I have been so lucky. Some time ago I had an impression that the collection ought to be worth close on two thousand pounds, and I had it specially insured for that amount. Well, one lives and learns. I came to go over some of the finest things in it—things that my father had got, and I didn't like the look of a good many of them. I got in one of the best experts in London and he confirmed my opinion. The poor old chap had been taken in. Collectors were not so scientific in his day as they are now. Nearly all his best things, the things that give a real money value to a collection, were forgeries. If that collection was worth a thousand pounds, that is every penny it was worth. It was insured for two thousand, and the insurance people will pay up like lambs. Consequently, I am one thousand pounds to the good on that burglary. I shall begin collecting again with a better system of arrangement, and thoroughly enjoy it. As I said to the police, if I could find the man who stole that collection I'd shake him by the hand and thank him. It might be my duty to get him six months afterwards, but that's another matter."

I said, and indeed I thought, that this was very extraordinary.

I went on chatting with him for about a quarter of an hour, and, as I expected, the name of the insurance people slipped out. It was a good, solid company. As I got up to go, I said: "Now, Stanwick, may I speak one word to you seriously?"

"You may," he said. "But if it is what I think it is, you will be wasting your time."

"That," I said, "I cannot help. I must do what I believe to be my duty. I want you to reconsider the case of Mrs Gimbrell. She had nothing to do with that woman Sander's transgressions, and it is not right or fair that she should be punished for them."

"How am I to know that she had nothing to do with them? The women were cousins, and it's my belief that it was a put-up thing between them. You've been taken in, as you always are I've been taken in too, but I don't give the same person the chance to take me in twice."

"I assure you, you are wrong. I have made mistakes, but I've made none about Mrs Gimbrell. The woman is honest now and is doing her best to make her husband honest. You must take her back."

"Sorry I can't oblige you, Dix, but I won't."

"Remember," I said, "that the unjust and tyrannical are often punished, even in this world."

"I don't know about that. According to you, I was unjust and tyrannical in sacking a woman for combining with another one to swindle my firm. According to you, I ought to have been struck dead or something in that line. As a matter of fact, a few days later I get this burglary which suits me down to the ground, and puts a thousand pounds in my pocket. Keep that kind of thing for your sermons, Dix. I am a businessman and it has no effect with me. When the punishment comes I may change my mind."

I appeared depressed as I left him, and he told me to cheer up. As soon as I was out in the street I did cheer up. I very seldom laugh, but I smiled as I walked back to my house in Bloomsbury. Undoubtedly it might appear to a superficial observer that I had lost the game. On the contrary, I was absolutely certain that I had won it.

On the following day I went down to see Mrs Gimbrell. She was despondent and inclined to grumble. "What's the good of keeping strite?" she asked. "That's the plain question I'd like you to answer me, Mr Dix. It seems you get the sack just the same one way as the other, and how am I to get took on anywhere else? I feel like chucking it, and letting Alf try his hand at the old game again. It mayn't have been right, but there was some money in it while it lasted."

"Mrs Gimbrell," I said, "this rebellious spirit must be checked, natural though it may be. You would not speak like that if you knew what had happened. Yesterday I had a few words with Mr Stanwick on your behalf, and I promise you that within a very few days he will send for you and give you again the same work that you had before."

Mrs Gimbrell was voluble in her thanks. I hope that my reader will not think that I had any intention of deceiving the poor woman. I could see through to the end of the game, and the end of the game was to be checkmate for Mr Stanwick. He is a man who believes in luck, and I felt sure that when the blow came he would recall my words and change his mind about Mrs Gimbrell.

On my return to my house I did up the Stanwicks' collection of stamps in a neat parcel, and wrote on it in a large, printed hand, "Taken in error from Hedley Mount, Wimbledon Common, residence of Mr Algeron Stanwick." I put this under another cover, directed in a similar hand to the insurance company, and took the next train with it to Northampton. From Northampton I sent off my parcel and returned to London again.

A few days later I made it my business to meet Mr Stanwick as he was going out to lunch. We lunched together and he did his best to appear cheerful. He is a man who cannot help bragging of his good luck, but where possible, keeps his misfortunes to himself, especially if they are of a kind to render him ridiculous. During lunch he said:

"I am going to put a funny question to you. After you left me the other day, did you make any attempt to discover who it was that took my stamp collection? I know you are in touch with all these blackguards, and they might tell you things that they wouldn't tell everybody."

"They do," I said. "But I made no such attempt. I never do police work. If I ever tried anything of the kind, my influence for good would be lost at once. Why do you ask?"

"I don't know," he said meditatively, "I had some sort of wild idea in my head, but there can be nothing in it. Let's talk about something else."

Towards the close of lunch he said: "By the way, you wanted me to take that Mrs Gimbrell back again. Do you think she's honest?"

"I am sure she is," I said.

"Yes, but you wouldn't bet on it. Money talks. Would you be prepared to renew your guarantee for as long as she worked for me?"

"Certainly I would, and be glad of the chance."

"Well then," he said, "next time you see her you can send her up, and I'll see what can be done. I suppose you won't leave me any peace till I do take her back."

In this guess of my intentions he was perfectly correct. At the moment of recording this incident Mrs Gimbrell is still working for the firm, and has had employment from them for the last two years.

Naturally from the higher point of view I regard all this with great satisfaction. At the same time I must confess that it was certainly not business.

V

THE REWARDS OF PERSEVERANCE

I was about to pay my usual spring visit to Brussels. At this time of the year the Belgian Paris is particularly attractive to me, and, as I have already explained, the man who buys my diamonds lives in Brussels. As a rule I combine business with pleasure. The trouble was that on this occasion I had no diamonds. They are a form of property in which I like to deal, small, valuable, and—apart from their setting—difficult of identification. I remove the settings myself and throw them away. It may possibly be remembered that some years ago a man made a curious find on the Underground Line between Gower Street and King's Cross. He found what I had intentionally lost. I never attempt to get the melting-pot value of settings. The risk is quite out of proportion to the profit. If I get a few hundred pounds' worth of diamonds I am content. In this business, as on the Stock Exchange and elsewhere, people lose money through opening their mouths too wide. It is a rare thing for spring to come round and find me with nothing in my pocket to show to my good friend, the merchant in Brussels; but it was the case this year. I had been busy on other matters. I now began to think out some simple way of supplying the deficiency.

As I turned the pages of the *Morning Post* my eye was arrested by the announcement that a marriage had been arranged and would take place on the third of the following month, between General Welbrand, C.B., and Madeline, youngest daughter of Sir Charles Wray, Bart., J.P., M.P., of Ditton Field, Withycomb, in the county of Norfolk.

The advertisement was of interest to me because I know something of Ditton Field. Ikey once had to admit a defeat there. He was not detected, he simply had to give the thing up after five hours' hard work. During those five hours he assured me that he had been within an ace of being shot by spring guns several times over. He came away with absolutely nothing but a sprig of rosemary which, so he said, he had picked in the garden to remember Sir Charles by. He attempted to make the journey back to London, without a ticket, in a goods truck, and, owing to a miscalculation on his part, got some fifty miles in the opposite direction before he had a chance to escape. He has always spoken to me with some bitterness of his Ditton Park experiences.

I thought it might be interesting to hear what Ikey had to say on the subject now. I met him coming out of the reading-room, and he began at once. He never fails to read the Fashionable Intelligence. "And," he said, "the presents will be 'numerous and costly,' as the papers say. The Duke, her godfather, is good for a diamond tiara anyhow, and there is not the ghost of a chance for anybody—not a blooming earthly. Mind, I wouldn't take it or think about taking it if there were. I'm a reformed character as you know. Still, it is funny to think of all that good stuff lying about loose in the big billiard-room, 'so near and yet so far,' as the song says."

"Ah, Ikey," I said, "you'd better give up thinking about it. The best way to avoid temptation is to put the subject from one's mind altogether."

"Who's talking about temptation? Look here, Mr Dix, I might want the moon, and I might talk about the moon, but I shouldn't take it. For the same reason I shouldn't take the stuff from that billiard-room. Do you think I don't know? I went back there when the second daughter was married. They'd two detectives in the house for days before, and those wedding presents were never left for one moment night or day. Even if you could get into the house, you couldn't do anything, without you chanced making a swinging job of it. No, you needn't get nervous about me, Mr Dix, you've shown me the error, and you can depend on my word that I keep out of it for the future."

I could not in the least depend on his word; indeed, this was only a few months before, under the influence of a little drink, he rejoined his old companions and fell back into evil courses. I said to him now that he would do well to show a less boastful spirit, and pointed out the need of constant watchfulness.

When I got home I sat down to think the thing out. On the face of it it was clearly a case for drugs. The difficulty would be to administer them. Sir Charles would undoubtedly deal with a first-class firm, and the detectives supplied would be good men. They would go straight to the house on their arrival and would probably not leave the house, certainly would not leave the grounds, until their work was over. It seemed to me that my only way of getting access to them would be to obtain employment of some kind in Sir Charles's household. This meant the assumption of a disguise, a careful sustaining of a new character, and the writing of a few forged testimonials. Frankly, I didn't like it.

The disguise and the *alias* are dangerous weapons, and, where they do not succeed perfectly, they damage the man who uses them. It was extremely improbable that I should be able to get a post as an indoor servant; my best chance would be as a groom or common labourer. That would mean that I should have to live and to work as a man of that class would. To all of this I had the strongest objection, but I did not see what else I could do.

About a week before the marriage took place I went down to Withycomb and put up at the hotel there, in my own name. They warned me that all their rooms were taken for the night before the wedding, and if I stayed on then I should have to go to the village beer house; a place where I felt sure I should be supremely uncomfortable. Things were not going well. However, I looked about the place and found an empty cottage standing by itself some way outside the village. It struck me that this would be an ideal spot in which to effect my disguise. The next afternoon I entered that cottage as Constantine Dix, a gentleman from London, interested in geology, and on the search for specimens. That was the description I had given of myself at the hotel. The small bag that I carried contained all that I wanted in the way of a disguise. I left the cottage, half an hour later, as William Bradshal, gardener, highly respectable, but in indifferent health, with a good place to go to in two months' time, and urgently in need of a job to tide him over until then.

Again my bad luck followed me. The Scotch head gardener, a sulky-looking brute, would neither hear my story nor look at my testimonials. He repeated that he didn't want anybody and there was nothing for me. When I lingered and persisted in trying to tell my story, he said that he would give me just one minute to get out of the place, and that after that he had a very good terrier. I got out of the place within my minute and I made a mental note of that head gardener. It is not a crime to ask for work, and I had not begged. It seemed to me that he was a man who should one day have a lesson. I heard afterwards that special orders had been given that no strangers were to be allowed to hang about the place under any pretext whatever. Also, I fancy that no servant was ever taken on there without a personal character and a prolonged and searching examination into his past history.

The only thing now before me was to go back to my cottage, resume the character of Mr Constantine Dix, pay my hotel bill, and go home. But I could not bring myself to go just yet. I had taken a good look at the house when I was trying for work there, and I determined to have another look at it that night.

My bedroom at the hotel was on the first floor, and gave me a fairly easy chance of coming and going at night-time without detection. I climbed down from the window at about three the next morning, the rainwater pipe affording me sufficient assistance. The billiard-room at Ditton Field is a big room, built out by Sir Charles at one side of the house. There are no rooms over it and one end of it is in view from a narrow country lane. I went down the lane, looked and saw nothing. Not one spark of light came from the window. I was just coming to the conclusion that Ikey had made a mistake, and that no watch was kept over the presents at night, when I noticed smoke curling up from the chimney of the room. A fire then was burning there, and a fire would not be burning there unless someone was sitting up. The lane comes within ten yards of the end of the billiard-room, and the fence offered no difficulties. I went with the utmost caution, feeling for places for my feet with my fingers, to be sure that there were no wires. I did not find anything of the kind, and possibly Ikey exaggerated the dangers he had gone through to cover a clumsy failure. I came close up to the wall and reached up my hand to the window above me. It was steel-shuttered. Even if there had been no detective inside it would have been impossible to tackle without burglars' tools, and these I never carry. As my fingers touched the steel I suddenly felt it begin to move under them. I had no time to get away, nor did it seem to me that there was much necessity. I stood close under the window, pressed tight against the wall, and it was a dark night. A man might have opened the window and looked out without seeing me.

Presently a man did look out. The steel shutter moved slowly up, and the light streaming out on the grass, showed me a man's shadow. Then the window was pushed up. I could smell coffee and hear the chink of the cup. Then the man leaned out. I heard a match strike and I could smell his cigarette. He smoked that cigarette out of the window, and made it last for twenty minutes, during which time I remained motionless and made no sound. Then, to my great relief, the window was shut, and the steel shutter, operated from the inside, came slowly down. I went back to my hotel with the comfortable feeling of a man who, after encountering difficulty and disappointment, at last sees his way clear.

The ascent to my bedroom was not easy but I managed it without noise or mishap of any kind. Before I went to sleep, I reviewed the situation. The billiard-room was left in charge of a detective all night. Once at least in the course of the night, he opened the window and renewed the air in the room. That would be quite natural, especially as a close atmosphere would tend to make him sleepy. I felt that I could depend upon it; he might very possibly leave the window open all the time he was there, but ten minutes would be quite enough for me. During those minutes locks and bolts and shutters for all practical purposes would have ceased to exist, and it would simply be a question whether he or I were the more intelligent and capable man. Without prejudice, I felt assured that I was.

The window in question was something between six and seven feet from the ground. I gathered that at this end of the room was the usual raised platform, and that the top of a table placed on it would come very near to the bottom of the window. I was certain that this was the platform end of the room, because the window at the other end came some three feet lower down, as I had noticed when I was trying to talk to the head gardener. On the table would be placed the detective's refreshments; I should hardly have heard the chink of the cup and smelled the coffee so distinctly if they had been further back in the room. Probably, the billiard-table would be covered over, and the display of presents would already be arranged on it, on the eve of the wedding, in readiness for the reception to follow. I should be able to see into the room, once the shutter was up, either by climbing a tree in the lane ten yards away, or on the grass under the window by standing on something that would increase my height (six feet) by one foot. I proposed to drug the detective, either through his cigarette or his coffee. I had not yet decided which, and both presented difficulties. It was clear to me that there was no point in my remaining longer at the hotel, and my absence might tend to avert suspicion. I decided to leave next morning and return on the eve of the wedding on my motor, with my plans completed.

Next day I was back in London, buying a few trifles which I required to make clean work of it. Ikey would not have made clean work of it. He would have tried a surprise entry through the window, calculating on frightening the detective into silence with a revolver, or overpowering him before he could call or get at the bell-push. And it would not have answered. I fear he would have made, as he said, a swinging job of it. Personally, I hate violence. I hate bloodshed. If diamonds could only be got by such means, I would leave them alone and take something else. I happen by chance to be tall and broad, and of considerable muscular strength. A man like Ikey has a great admiration for that, says so plainly, and turns me sick; I feel as if I were being treated as a prize beast. It has happened sometimes—inevitably, I suppose—in the course of my work among very rough characters that I have had to resort to the lowest methods. It has become necessary for me to get a man out of a room, or to hit him hard. One does it if it is necessary, but one might be spared the disgust of being congratulated. The mental qualities are higher. When my mind prevails against the mind of another, I feel some satisfaction, but I try to keep myself from that silly vanity which leads to an ambitious and fatal attempt to achieve the impossible. I remember that the spiritual qualities are higher still. Among the worst and the hardest I have picked out now and again the most hopeless case of all. Friends have pleaded with me not to waste my efforts, and others have ridiculed me, but I have stuck to my man, and after repeated failures have brought him to a new life. There lies my spiritual triumph, but that too brings me no vanity—only steady submission where struggle is useless— submission to that which is fore-ordained. For there are some whom we think lost that are meant for the rescue, and there are some—myself amongst them—who have a good place among men, whose virtues are credited, whose fame is unspotted; and these are to go on to the end without hope. It is a subject to which I had intended hardly to allude, and one on which I will not dwell.

I told my housekeeper, Mrs Pethwick—an elderly but invaluable woman—that I was going to take the motor down to Brighton for a couple of days. She saw that my bag was packed, and I gave her an ordinary leather-covered ink-pot to put in it— one of those that fasten with a couple of springs. The word "ink" was stamped in gold on the top of it, but the liquid inside was not ink. It looked like it in the ink-pot, but the colour was really dark brown. You would have found on searching my motor-car three feet of fine metal tube, and an india-rubber bulb, and you would have concluded that they had some connection with the mechanism of the motor; you would have been wrong. I had my big pocket knife in my pocket. I was starting off to steal diamonds of great value, watched by a detective, and this was all the apparatus I took with me for that purpose. I also took my special cigarette—that cigarette which will be the last I ever put to my lips—but this was for afterwards, in case of failure and capture. I reached Norwich in time for dinner. I admit that it is not essential to take Norwich on the way from London to Brighton, but I had not told Mrs Pethwick that I was going by the most direct route. I had merely said that I was going to Brighton; and I did go there ultimately.

At dinner, somewhat, I fear, to the disgust of the waiter, I drank one bottle of soda water, and after dinner I slept for an hour in the smoking-room. I was extremely pleased that I was able to get to sleep quite easily. It showed me that my nerves were in good order. I left the hotel at about ten, and drove my car easily along in the direction of Withycomb, which is perhaps twenty-four or twenty-five miles from Norwich. The country about here is not very populous and the inhabitants go to bed early. I felt quite secure in running my motor into a field and leaving it hidden behind a couple of stacks. From this point I went on foot to Ditton Field, taking with me the apparatus which I have already described.

I could see from the lane that the steel shutter of the window of the billiard-room was not quite closed; the lower three inches were open and the window was open behind it. I thought it likely that it would remain like this for the rest of the night. Of course this meant that I could not command a view of the room from a tree in the lane. I had to get to the grass just in front of the window and find something to stand upon which would bring my eyes on a level with the narrow opening. I was in no particular hurry. I explored the place a little with the greatest care, and found in an unlocked potting shed a solid wine-case which I thought would serve my purpose. I kept away from the lodge, the gardener's cottage, and the house itself, as much as possible in case a dog might discover me. Dogs were what I was principally afraid of that night. I do not mean that I was afraid of a dog attacking me; a dog that did that would die before any great harm was done to me. It was the noise that I wished to avoid. I brought the packing-case up with me to my position in the lane, and from there I watched the narrow strip of light at the bottom of the window for any sign of movement. The night was pitch dark, and it had now come on to rain hard. For an hour or more I saw nothing, and then I got a glimpse of a moving hand and a shirt cuff and something that looked to me as if it might be the base of a coffee-pot. The moment for action had now arrived. I fixed the india-rubber bulb on one end of my long metal tube, dipped the other end into that inkpot and released the bulb. The tube was now charged with the drug which was to do the work for me. I put my packing-case in position on the grass just in front of the window with the tube beside it, mounted the case and got my first view of the interior of the room. At the table near the window sat the detective — a pale young man, with a plaintive eye, who sat munching ham sandwiches in the ruminative manner of an ordinary cow. His cup of innocuous and sleep-dispelling coffee was by his side. The display of presents was already arranged on the billiard-table and other tables in the room. From the position in which I stood it would have been quite easy for me to have reached the coffee cup with my metal tube, and by squeezing the bulb, to have discharged the poison into it. But the detective would have seen me, and the snare should not be laid in sight of the bird. It was necessary for me to attract his attention elsewhere.

I went round to the other end of the billiard-room, opened the nail file in my pocketknife and drew it once, sharply, across the steel shutter, immediately returning to my position by the opposite window. I had reflected that this course might be disastrous. The detective might have gone straight to the electric bell which would have summoned his comrade. But I was right in supposing that he would be reluctant to disturb his friend's sleep until he knew beyond question that there was some need for him. The sound which I had made on the steel shutter was suspicious, and would attract him to that end of the room, but he would wait for something further before he rang. Looking through the window I could see him at the further end of the room with his back to me, listening intently. He had already got his revolver out. Leisurely, though with proper care, I put one end of my tube through the window till it was immediately over the coffee cup, and pressed the bulb very slowly and gently. I fancy that a quarter of an hour or twenty minutes must have elapsed before the detective decided that he might return and finish his coffee, and that the sound which he had heard was probably nothing more than a twig of some tree, scratched against the shutter by the wind.

After this for a while things seemed to go very slowly. The detective took his coffee in small sips at considerable intervals. When one has absolutely nothing to do, a cup of coffee is an incident. One prolongs it; it breaks the monotony. He finished it at last, lit his pipe and picked up a journal devoted to the interests of the amateur photographer.

The action of a drug depends to some extent on the idiosyncrasy of the person who takes it. With my friend the action was slow, but it came at last. His pipe fell to the floor with a crash, and he sprang to his feet. He had actually been to sleep. He was still drowsy. If he had been wise he would have rung the bell at once. I now crouched low under the ledge of the window for I knew what would happen. The steel shutter flew up, and the man thrust his head out. The cold night air, he thought, would dispel his sleepiness. He had relit his pipe. In a few seconds it fell at my feet, and his shadow disappeared. I mounted my packing-case in an instant and saw him trying to make his way to the bell. He swayed and staggered in the intoxication of the drug. As he neared the bell and had his hand out toward it he collapsed, went over, and lay like a log. I waited for a little to see if the noise of his fall had aroused anybody, and then put my hands on the ledge of the window and pulled myself into the room. My attention was attracted first by a square morocco case, of apparent magnificence and emblazoned with a crest and initials. The card upon it signified that it was the gift of the Duchess of Tadcaster. I opened it, and found that it contained six small silver coffee-spoons, total value nine shillings. I could not help writing upon the card that this was really very shabby of Her Grace, and then I got on to serious business, going for diamonds only. It was, without exception, the biggest haul I ever made in my life. The mere removal of the stones from their settings took me days of work afterwards. Two South African magnates had been particularly handsome on this occasion. I then turned my attention to the detective. I undid his collar and put him in a better position. He murmured something about being "done for," but I think he was really unconscious, and supposed that he was talking to the other detective. I let myself down from the window and went back to the lane.

As I took a last look at the house a police whistle sounded shrilly—I heard the continued whirr of more than one electric bell, and window after window sprang into life. I saw, of course, what had happened. The other detective had entered to take his comrade's place the moment after I had left. I got out of the lane at once into a field. On these occasions it is always supposed that the burglar will be obliging enough to confine himself strictly to streets or roads or other places patrolled by the police. This is not always the case. I got back to my motor in safety, put my diamonds, roughly tied up in a couple of handkerchiefs, under one of the seats and started off. As soon as I was in the road, I got on to my top speed at once, and after that I felt perfectly secure. A policeman did challenge me, but this was forty miles away, and I think he merely wanted my name and address because my lamps were not lit. But I was busy at the time and could not stop. Naturally I was very late in arriving at Brighton, but, as I explained to the old couple who look after my cottage there, the best motor-cars break down sometimes.

VI

LOST PROPERTY

I was delivering an address in the open air one Sunday when I noticed among the small congregation who had gathered round me, a man whom I knew, of the name of James Barker. Barker was a criminal whom I had reclaimed some two years before, and for the last two years I knew that he had been living an honest life. He was a clever cabinet-maker and commanded good wages. His original lapse had been due more to the effects of bad company and to the desire to get rich quickly than to any congenital criminal instinct in him. He not infrequently attended at the meetings which I conducted, and I noticed that now he was following my address with every appearance of the keenest interest. I was speaking on the subject of restitution, and pointing out that it is not enough to repent of the wrong we have done any man, but that we should strive, so far possible, to make amends, and if he has suffered loss from us, to make that loss good.

Barker still lingered when the rest had dispersed, and I went up and spoke to him. We chatted of the weather and his work. He was fairly prosperous and had nothing to complain of. But I could see that there was something on his mind, and I was not surprised when he said that he would like to have a few words with me on a matter of business, if I knew of any place where we could go. I took him to a respectable coffeehouse where I was known, and there, over a cup of tea and a pipe, he told me rather a curious story. It was the story of the last theft he had committed.

He was at that time temporarily employed by a builder at Lufbridge in Lincolnshire. While he was at work he made the acquaintance of the second housemaid at the Towers. The Towers was a house of fairly good style, and the residence in the country of Mr Augustus Havant, diamond merchant, of Hatton Garden. The housemaid, Mary, was a pretty girl, and I understood that Barker's attentions to her were at first entirely for her own sake, and not with any idea of extracting useful information. But the girl, like many servants, was a little given to bragging of the splendours of the house where she was employed. She talked, and Barker listened. As he said to me now in the coffee-room, it seemed to him as if the whole thing had been done up in a parcel and slipped into his hand, and that he would be a fool not to take it. He learned that Havant was in the habit of spending Saturday to Monday at the Towers and that the house was generally full of visitors at these times. Mrs Havant and some of her friends were deeply interested in diamonds, and Havant would frequently bring down a few specimens. It happened sometimes when he was entertaining his Jewish friends that a little business would be done, and the diamonds that came down from London in Havant's pocket would go back in the pocket of another dealer. There was a good safe in the gun-room where Havant kept any precious stones that he had brought down with him. James Barker laid his plans with some care, but he made far too much noise in opening the safe. He got away with a paper of diamonds of great value and importance, but he had been seen, and he knew it. The robbery was committed at about half-past four in the morning, and Barker succeeded in getting into the workmen's train which leaves Lufbridge at five, He was careful to enter the station at the last moment, dashed across the platform and jumped into a first-class carriage. As soon as the train had started he felt that he had jumped into a trap. Undoubtedly telegrams would be sent to all the stations up the line, and he would be arrested as soon as he stepped out of the carriage. As a matter of fact, he had no sooner stepped on to the platform at Sandys Junction than he was tapped on the shoulder. He had a perfect story to tell; he had been detained working overtime at Lufbridge, and this was the first train by which he had been able to get back. He knew nothing of Havant, but thought one of the housemaids there was a pretty girl. He was sorry to hear there had been a burglary, but he had nothing whatever to do with it, and was an honest working-man, as his bag of tools would testify. At his own request he was searched most carefully and no diamonds were found on him. He told me that they did not keep him more than a few minutes, and that it had been worth a good cigar and a pint of bitter to him.

"There you are, Barker," I said, "that incident shows that theft is not only wicked but in nine cases out of ten foolish as well. You take away a man's diamonds, and an hour later you have to throw them out of a carriage window to save your own skin."

"Begging your pardon, sir, but what's all this about carriage windows? I never threw the diamonds out of the window. I took one of the carriage cushions, cut a slit in the bottom of it, slipped in the diamonds, and sewed the slit up again. I can use a needle and thread as well as any woman. I left the diamonds in the carriage behind me, meaning to come back for them one day when things had quieted down. I could have made pals with the carriage cleaner and got them again somehow. But, as you know, before that time came I met with you and decided to chuck all crooked work. Well, the thing's been in my mind a good bit, and what you were saying in the Park today goes home. I'm not going to put my neck into a noose, I shouldn't be any the better for penal servitude, but it does seem to me that there might be some way of telling that man Havant where his diamonds are. It's restitution, there's sense and reason in it."

"It is the greatest pity," I said, "that you did not bring this story to me before. It would have been perfectly easy to have restored the diamonds to their rightful owner then. You could have sent him a typewritten and unsigned letter, saying where the diamonds were, and you might have safely left him to have done the rest. But now it's too late."

"Why is it too late?"

"I happened to be travelling on that local branch between Lufbridge and Sandys Junction only a few days ago. The carriages had been recently, I should say very recently, re-upholstered. By this time the cushion in which you hid the diamonds is probably burnt or sold, and it would be impossible to trace it."

It was not quite easy at first to make James Barker see that the cushion could not be traced. I thought it advisable to re-inforce my argument by saying that after all perhaps this was for the best. If Havant had received that typewritten letter, he would have communicated with the police, and they would have remembered, doubtless, the man whom they had searched at Sandys. "I am anxious, Barker," I said, "particularly anxious, that nothing should happen which would throw you again, either in prison or out of it, into the society of criminals. Your desire to make restitution is most laudable, but the opportunity has gone past."

He left me after some further talk, quite decided to do nothing further in the matter but not entirely satisfied.

Personally, I was quite satisfied. I thought it over as I walked back to my house in Bloomsbury. The story I had told James Barker was perfectly true. I had been on the local line between Lufbridge and Sandys, and I had noticed that the carriages had been recently re-upholstered, and that the rolling stock generally looked much smarter than it had done a year before. It was possible, of course, that the loose cushions in the first-class carriages had been merely re-covered. In that case the diamonds must have already been found. If, on the other hand, the cushions had been sold, there was clearly a chance for me.

I did not believe that the diamonds had been found.

Working men and women who deal with the re-covering of cushions and the re-upholstering of railway carriages are not experts in precious stones. The lucky finder would have taken the diamonds at once to the nearest jeweller to find out what they were, and what there value was. The thing would have been in all the newspapers; I should certainly have heard of it I went down to Sandys Junction and had a chat with the guard of one of the trains, an old acquaintance of mine. It was natural enough for me to say that I often wondered when one of those carriages was re-upholstered what was done with the old stuff.

"Well, the contractor takes that, of course, burns most of it, I expect. He might be able to make something out of loose cushions, ripping off the old covers and putting on new, but I couldn't say for certain."

This was not very good news. If the cushions were burnt the diamonds were lost; if the cushions were recovered the diamonds were found. And in either case I was wasting my time. However, I got the name of the contractor, a local man, and managed to find out from him what had happened. He had kept none of the stuff himself. He said proudly that he saw the state of it, and that it was not worth his attention. I said with innocent wonder that it must have been difficult for him to find a customer.

"Bless you I could have found a hundred, by putting my head out of the window and whistling. There's always somebody to buy anything, so long as the price is right. That lot went to a marine store-dealer in Yarmouth."

I hesitated whether it would be worthwhile to follow the matter up further, but railway journeys amuse me, and on the following day I went to Yarmouth. I had not got the dealer's name, and had not wished to arouse suspicion unnecessarily by asking for it. So I did not hit on the right man the first time, or the second, or the third, but I got him in the end. And when I reminded him of that lot of stuff out of the railway carriages that he had bought, he swore very heartily. He had paid too much for it, he said.

"And what do you do with that kind of thing?" I asked.

"Destroy the worst of it and make up the rest. Some of the loose cushions I sold just as they were, and a lot of them are still on my hands. You can have them at your own price, if you like. They take up a lot of room, and I should be glad to be quit of them."

I said that I doubted if it would be worth my while, but there could be no harm in looking. His son took me upstairs to an attic where they were stored. I turned every one of them over, and not one of them had the slit sewn up in the leather underside that Barker had described to me.

The hunt was beginning to be a long one, and I was by no means certain of finding my quarry in the end. Again I thought of giving the whole thing up and going back to London for some work which would be more certainly remunerative. But I pictured the diamonds as Barker had described them to me, and could not bring myself to leave any chance. I went down to the dealer, asked what he wanted for the cushions and made a point of grumbling at the price. "You are likely to keep them," I said, "if that's what you want. The only people who would buy at that rate are safely shut up in the asylums."

"Well," said the dealer, "I'm asking you just the same that I got for the other lot that I sold."

"I'll bet a sovereign that's a lie," I said.

"Right," said the dealer, "I take that. I'm not over and above fond of being called a liar. This'll cost you something. If you'll just step into my office, I'll get the book out."

He showed me the book with a note of the transaction in it. He was quite correct, and I handed over my sovereign with a crestfallen air. I went away with the information that I wanted. The man who had bought the cushions was named Solway, and was a proprietor of bathing-machines and pleasure-boats at Hayley-on-Sea. The thing was becoming ridiculous. I fully expected that when I reached Hayley-on-Sea I should find that the enterprising Solway had shipped the cushions across to Holland for conversion into beef-tea or liqueurs. There was no trouble in finding Solway. Solway advertised himself at the station, and at my hotel, and on the beach. He was, it seemed, a prop and pillar of Hayley-on-Sea, and was looked upon with respect. The head waiter at the hotel expressed the opinion that Solway was "a warm man," and wished, with a sigh, that he had as many shillings as Solway had sovereigns. But there was no pride about the Solway family. The old man sat at the receipt of custom in a shed by the bathing-machines. His sons took visitors out in the pleasure-boats; his daughters had under their care a wide range of skimpy towels and excessive bathing-costumes. There was also a Solway nephew, but his only occupation was to fetch beer for the other Solways. They were a genial family and they drank a good deal of beer. I had not the least difficulty in getting into conversation with Solway, and in looking over the piled cushions of his many pleasure-boats.

I touched one of them with my stick, and said that it looked just as if it might have come out of a railway carriage.

Solway emphatically desired the Lord to bless his soul if this was not a funny thing. In effect they were railway cushions, and he told me with much detail how they were procured. I had taken a season ticket for his rotten bathing machines, and was in consequence a person to be treated with courtesy, including conversation if required.

I said that I was surprised that it was worth his while to buy cushions of that kind; probably every one of them had been cut about by some mischievous railway traveller at some time or another, Solway said he did not think so; the cushions were in fair condition.

I immediately bet him a shilling that the one which I touched had a slit in it somewhere. If the slit were sewn up it was to count just the same. He took my bet, and I lost. I repeated the bet about two other cushions, and lost again.

Then Solway desired the Lord to bless his soul again, if he was going on taking money in this foolish way. He had had the pick of the cushions when he bought them, and he had not had them for long. If they had been shabby they would not have done for his business. As a matter of fact, only one of the cushions that he had bought was at all damaged; that had a slit on the under side, and he knew that was not in the pile I was looking at, because he had given it away, He added that it seemed as if I was kind of interested in cushions.

"Ah," I said, "we were talking about you the other night up at the hotel, and they gave you rather a different character there."

"What do you mean? " asked Solway.

"Well, there was a man there in the bar who said that old Solway had never given to anybody in the whole course of his life."

Solway grinned appreciatively. He took this as a welcome compliment, but felt compelled to admit that he had been flattered beyond his deserts. He had not given away much, and that was a fact. He would not have been what he was, and where he was, if he had parted with things too readily. But it was true about the cushion.

"Then," I said, "give me a chance to get back some of the money that I have just been losing to you. I shall see that chap up at the hotel again tonight, and I think I could get a bet on with him. Of course he would want to know the name of the man to whom you gave the cushion. He wouldn't merely take your word for it."

Solway said proudly that he supposed his word was about as good as the Bible oath of most people, but he had no objection to giving the name. It was a funny thing, but he had given that cushion to a trade rival, if you could call him a rival. He was a poor old chap named Marsh, who had got but one boat, and his living depended on it.

There was not the least probability that Marsh would have parted with the cushion. I felt now that I could put my hand on it at any time, and, moreover, the sea air and my bathe had made me hungry. I went back to lunch. After lunch I went down to the beach, and made an enquiry or two. No, I could not have Marsh's boat. The old man was taking two young gents out for a sail in it. They went out every afternoon when it was fine. It did not look particularly fine this afternoon. A few drops of rain fell. I bought a newspaper, and betook me to a shelter to read. From this point I noticed that the astute Solway was refusing to let his sailing boats go out.

The storm is still well remembered at Hayley-on-Sea, and, of course, the disaster to Marsh's boat was in all the papers next day. Nobody quite knew how it happened, but not one of the three lives was saved. It might have happened in many ways. The boat was found floating keel uppermost. And somewhere, at the bottom of the English Channel, there is a railway carriage cushion containing a packet of valuable diamonds.

Had I gone straight on to Marsh directly after leaving Solway, those diamonds would now have been in my possession, or would have been sold by me to my friend in Brussels. On such small chances do success and failure depend. In my own, as in many more desirable occupations, long and patient work and abilities far beyond the average are impotent against a whim of destiny. I do not wonder that I am a fatalist, but it is strange to me that there are those who are not fatalists.

This was not one of the occasions on which I decided to drink. It was necessary for me to keep such powers as I have at their best for some immediately remunerative work. A series of thefts took place at Hayley-on-Sea, during the next week. Solway, for instance, lost a couple of hundred pounds of his savings. The local paper assured us that the police had a clue. I have reason to believe that they had not.

VII

HOLIDAY WORK

I had not meant to stop at Lunford at all, but to go straight on to town, but my accumulators gave out, and I had to wait to get them recharged. After all, it only meant adding one day to the pleasant week's holiday which I had spent in touring.

That, at any rate, was what I thought at the time. As a matter of fact, it meant that my holiday was to be diversified by a little episode which may perhaps be classed as holiday work.

A few minutes after my arrival I was standing in the doorway of the hotel chatting with my host, a pleasant portly old-fashioned landlord—I regret the rapid disappearance of the type. As we were talking, a man passed us on a bicycle, with a small brown bag attached to the handle-bars. He was a man of about forty, thin and hard, with a worn black morning coat, a felt hat, and a rather solemn expression. The landlord jerked his thumb towards him. "There goes our Friday miracle," he said.

"And what's your Friday miracle?" I asked.

"Bartlett's—cocoa people, you know—have got a factory just outside the town."

"I passed it as I was driving in. Not much of a place, is it?"

"As you say, not much of a place at present. It's bigger than it was, and they say it's going to be bigger still. At present there's about seventy-five employed there. That man on the bicycle is Mr Bosworth, manager at the factory."

"He hardly looks the kind of chap to have the control of a business like that."

"No, no. He has nothing to do with the actual business; that is all run from the London office. He only manages this factory, and this factory is only one of about three in this county that Bartlett owns."

"I see. Well, where does his miraculousness come in?"

"It's a queer story, and you'll hardly believe it. The men and the girls at the factory are paid every Saturday. Every Friday afternoon Bosworth comes into the bank here, changes a cheque for the wages over the counter, and takes off the money with him in that brown bag. What do you make of that?"

"Nothing miraculous. It's the ordinary course of business, isn't it?"

The landlord clearly enjoyed the culmination of his story. "Yes," he said, "it's all ordinary so far; but now, sir, you listen to this. Supposing at some point between the bank and the factory you were to knock Mr Bosworth off his bicycle and go over his clothes and his brown bag, you might think that you'd be able to put your hand on the change for that cheque?"

"Certainly, if I were dishonest enough."

"Well," said the landlord, with triumph, "you wouldn't do anything of the kind. You wouldn't find one single penny on him. I have got good reason for what I say, because it has been tried twice. Once it was in the winter, and it was dark when he was returning. Two blackguards—the police have got them now—stretched a wire across the road. Bosworth came an almighty smash and was knocked senseless. They stole his Waterbury, and that was the only thing that they did get. About a year later another man who had noticed Bosworth's habits, and thought he saw a chance of helping himself, held him up on that lonely bit of road just before you get to the factory.

'What do you want?' says Bosworth. 'The week's wages,' says the man. 'Not got 'em,' says Bosworth. That didn't do with the man, and he had a set-to with Bosworth and looked into things for himself. There were a few stones in the brown bag, and there wasn't another thing. He didn't even get a Waterbury. Bosworth said he'd given up wearing watches, since they seemed only to put temptation in men's way."

"Yes, it's queer," I said, "but, of course, there can be only one explanation. At some point between the bank and the factory Bosworth hands over that money to another messenger."

The landlord shook his head. "That won't do, I think, sir. The two men who stopped him first stopped him just outside the town. He gets on his old bicycle at the bank, and nobody's ever seen him get off it between here and the factory."

"Then I give it up," I said, as I stepped back into the hall of the hotel. The neat black-silk manageress pushed up her window. "It's only for tonight, sir, that you require your room?"

Circumstances alter cases. I had certainly intended to remain for only one night, but the landlord's story had changed my mind. "I shall be here for a week," I said, "Possibly longer."

I took another look at the Bartlett's cocoa factory on the following day, and had some talk about it at a neighbouring beer house which did its business principally with Bartlett's workpeople. The manager, it appears, lived at the cottage adjoining the factory. He was married, and said to be henpecked. He had one child, a girl of ten. The family generally had the reputation of keeping themselves to themselves.

"I was wondering," I said to the girl at the beer house, "if people were allowed to see over the factory. It is the kind of thing that interests me rather."

"Well," she said, "you can but ask. There's the old woman coming down the road now."

She was a dumpy old woman, with a face full of character and determination. She carried a large basket.

"Where has she been?" I asked.

"Market. Saturday's market day at Lunford."

"She's back early."

"It's her usual time. Some of them will hang about all day doing nothing, but I will say she's not one of that sort."

On second thoughts I did not speak to Mrs Bosworth, nor did I go on to the factory. I went back to my hotel and thought it over. My idea was now that it was Mrs Bosworth, and not her husband, who brought the money from the bank to the factory. If that were the case the money arrived at the factory not on Friday but on Saturday morning, at the most half an hour before it was distributed in the form of wages. This was, from my point of view, much less promising. Had the money lain in Bosworth's cottage for one night I should have got it with no trouble, but if the money were only there for a few minutes in broad daylight I did not see how to manage it. It was by no means a bad idea on the part of the Bosworths that his Friday visit to the bank should act as a blind. Doubtless something or other was handed him over the counter, dummy bags in return for a dummy cheque, and in this way the attention of the people who wished to secure that money in transit would be confined to Bosworth himself, who never had the money. If I could read character from a face at all, it was Mrs Bosworth who had the cunning to plan this, and who preferred to take the responsibility of carrying the money herself. I remembered that I had been told that Bosworth was henpecked.

The irritating feature of the case was that I could only work on one day in the week. I waited in Lunford with what patience I might until the following Saturday, filling in my time by making notes and observations of some of the larger houses in the neighbourhood which might at some time be worth my attention. On Saturday I occupied myself solely in tracking Mrs Bosworth. She visited three shops, and she never went near the bank at all. One of the shops was a saddler's, kept by a man called Fitton. I did not quite see why she should go to a saddler's. Horses were employed at the factory, of course, but their equipment would have nothing to do with the wife of the manager. If Bosworth had kept a little pony and trap of his own I could have understood it; as it was I became suspicious. I left Mrs Bosworth when she started on her return journey, and came back to Fitton's. It was shortly after one when I returned to the shop, and I saw a neatly-dressed young man enter it and pass through the shop into the private part of the house. This, I said to myself, is the younger Mr Fitton. What does the younger Mr Fitton do? I answered that question for myself on the following Monday by calling at the bank on some purely bogus business. The younger Mr Fitton sat there and cast up columns. Now the whole thing was clear. The money was sent from the bank by Fitton to his father's house, and there Mrs Bosworth collected it. Having settled this to my satisfaction I paid my bill at the hotel, ran my car out, and drove back to London.

I was disgusted with the whole thing, and wished I had never embarked upon it. The sum at stake was little if anything over one hundred pounds. It seemed to me that it had involved, and would involve bother, and expense quite out of proportion to the prize. At the same time I did not like the idea of being outwitted by a simple old woman like Mrs Bosworth. What was I to do? I might have gone back on the following Saturday, followed Mrs Bosworth on her return to the factory, and in some lonely part of the road demanded the money from her. But she would not have given it up meekly; she would have fought for it. This course was quite impossible. Had she followed the estimable practice of many of the other old women of the district of looking in at the public-house for a glass of stout before her return journey, I could have made things more certain. As it was I had no chance of administering a drug. After long thought I decided on my knowledge of human nature that there would be just one brief space of time when that money would be less carefully guarded; this would be the short space after her arrival, and before the money was paid out. Once inside her house she would feel secure. I felt pretty certain there would be no servant there. She would put her big basket down on the kitchen table, and then run upstairs to take her bonnet off. That would be the moment.

I returned by train to Lunford on the following Saturday, and walked straight out to the factory. I was provided with nothing but a simple pyrotechnic arrangement intended to attract the attention of anybody in the Bosworth's cottage away from the spot where I should be operating. There were trees and high hedges coming close up to the cottage and providing admirable cover. I chose a position from which I could see the back door and a part of the kitchen through the window.

At her regular hour Mrs Bosworth returned, unlocked the back door and let herself in, leaving the door unlocked. She put her basket down on the kitchen table exactly as I had expected, but she did not go upstairs to take her bonnet off. She sat down on a Windsor chair and ate cheesecakes out of a paper bag. I slipped round to the front of the house, put an ordinary cracker in the long grass, and lit the touch-paper. I had just time to return to the back of the house when the explosion came. It happened exactly as I had supposed. She ran out of the kitchen to see what was the matter, and she was hardly out of it before I was in it. I had only a moment to get the money from the basket.

The basket contained tea, sugar, bacon, some remarkably pungent and impressive cheese, a piece of meat destined for Sunday's dinner, and no money at all.

I was back again in London at half-past three, reflecting on the danger of regarding deductions which are no more than possible as if they were absolutely inevitable.

I had been wrong from the very start. These provincial towns have to invent something interesting to save themselves from perishing of utter boredom. My landlord's talk about the Friday miracle was probably not entirely accurate. Certainly I should have had the sense to have seen that if Bosworth's Friday operations were merely a blind, they would not have been continued after this had twice been discovered. It was perfectly possible that on one occasion—I did not suppose there had been more than one—he had been stopped and no money had been found on him, but that did not prove that he never took money back from the bank to the factory. Why had I supposed that because the money was paid weekly it was drawn weekly from the bank? It was perfectly possible that Bosworth rendered a monthly account to his employers. Why had I supposed that the money was ever kept in the cottage at all? True, the business was run from the head office in London, but there would be correspondence with this office, and there would be accounts to be kept of time worked and of money paid. Obviously somewhere within the factory the manager would have his small office, and somewhere in the office there would be a safe.

I dislike safes. I never carry anything that the police could imagine to be a burglarious implement, and one cannot open a safe with a pocket-knife. The opening may sometimes be effected by explosives, and I was familiar with the process, but the noise is an objection. If I have to open a safe at all I prefer to open it with its key.

I was so much in doubt as to whether it would be worth my while to go on at all with this business, that I tossed a penny to decide it. If it came heads, I went to Lunford, if it came tails, I gave up Lunford and devoted myself to a jeweller's shop in Oxford on which I had long had my eye. The penny came down heads.

I now gave up loading myself with reproaches for my previous blunders in the matter, and began in a more steady and workmanlike way, no longer trusting to my own guesses founded on public-house tittle-tattle. I called at the factory on business, which, if it had been genuine, I should have taken to the central office. I asked to see Mr Bosworth, and was shown into his room. There stood the safe in the corner of it. I explained that I had a large order to place and had been told that Bartlett's could execute it, but judging from what I saw it was impossible, and I need not trouble the head office about it.

"Why impossible?" asked Bosworth.

"The place isn't big enough. I don't know what you turn out here."

"Perhaps a bit more than you think," said Mr Bosworth. "Have you got a quarter of an hour to spare? We've got some machinery here I should like you to see."

I looked at my watch doubtfully. "I might spare ten minutes," I said.

We left the office, the door of which shut with a spring lock. The moment we were outside I said, "I must go back for my hat. There is draught enough in these corridors to blow one's head off."

He opened the door again, remaining outside himself. I joined him in a couple of moments with my hat and an excellent impression in wax of the key of the safe. Then I wandered about and saw machinery which I did not understand. I had got up the subject of cocoa, and talked it like an expert. Bosworth said, if I did change my mind and give his firm the order, he hoped I would mention that it was in consequence of what he had shown me. I said I should be certain to do so.

After that everything was of a childish simplicity. I made a key myself, adapting one of the many, which I had in my possession. While Bosworth and his wife sat at supper the following Saturday evening, I was giving the yard dog of the factory his supper also. The yard dog's supper did not agree with it. The office was on the ground floor, and the window was carefully bolted, but it was one of these excellent catches for which every burglar who dislikes hard work must feel grateful. I pushed it back with my knife, and opened the safe. Although wages had been paid that day, I still found close on a couple of hundred pounds there, confirming me in my believe that Bosworth did draw the money monthly. His Friday visits to the bank might have been for the purpose of a blind, but were just as likely to be connected with business of his own. He was just the kind of man to save a few shillings, and bank it every week. But with the possession of the money these undetermined points ceased to have any interest for me. I walked slowly back across fields to the little village where I had left my motor-car, and from thence drove into London.

For the short address which I had promised to deliver on the following Sunday, I chose as a subject the danger of self-confidence. So often it happens that we can make our own failings serve as a help and a warning to others.

VIII

THE BELLASEN CROSS

I enquired one day of Alfred Gimbrell if he could tell me anything of Davis. Davis was a rough fellow, whose reform I had once in vain attempted. For several months I had heard nothing of him.

"Davis is put away," said Gimbrell. "Got it in the neck over the Bellasen business. A bit too much——" Gimbrell raised his elbow significantly.

"I see," I said. "And what was the Bellasen affair?"

"Well, it was in all the papers. The Bellasen cross, you know."

"I knew," I said, "that there was a cross composed of thirty magnificent emeralds in the possession of the Bellasen family. There is a description of it in most of the works on precious stones."

"Well," said Alfred, "it ain't in their possession now. Also there ain't no family—leastwise unless you call one woman a family. No more it is in Davis's possession neither. 'Tain't in anybody's possession. Ah, rum thing that was. And all through just a bit too much——" And once more Gimbrell gave his pantomimic representation of a man raising a glass to his lips.

His rather enigmatical remarks on the subject of the cross interested me. I thought it quite possible that it might become worth my own attention. I had always supposed that a jewel of immense value, an heirloom in the family as this was, would be kept in the bank, and I never trouble the strong rooms of London banks. But now I got Gimbrell to tell me the whole story as he knew it. It affords a good lesson to the intemperate.

The Bellasen cross was about two hundred years old, of French workmanship, and too large and heavy to be worn as a personal ornament. The Bellasens were always mightily proud of it, and when, chiefly through their own indiscretions, they were in comparatively low water, no attempt was ever made to get the necessary permission to sell the cross. This pride seems to have infected those who married into the family. At the time of this story there was not one Bellasen left. Lady Bellasen had been a Miss Crowe, the daughter of a small tradesman in Plymouth. It might have been supposed that she would have taken the first opportunity to convert the cross into its immense value in cash. But she was infected with the pride. Suggestions were made by the solicitors of her late husband, but were repudiated with contempt. She said flatly that she would not sell it to save herself from starvation.

She was in no danger whatever of starvation. But the land that the Bellasens still owned (and it had dwindled almost to nothing) had to be sold to pay her husband's debts. Lady Bellasen was left with an income of five hundred a year, and a cross of thirty emeralds, every one of which was worth more than her annual income.

Lady Bellasen buried herself in a box of a house at the bottom of a Yorkshire fell-side. The rent was low, and the scenery was magnificent. Old friends in London came down to see her from time to time. She had thoughts of adopting a boy, but gave up the idea, and began her history of the Bellasen family. She is still engaged on this laborious and monumental work, which promises to give almost as much trouble in the reading as it has done in the writing. But the convert ever shows the most

THE BELLASEN CROSS

enthusiasm; nobody was ever quite so keen about the Bellasens as this Miss Crowe was after she had taken their name.

She had a good safe in the dining-room of this house, and in that safe, without the slightest fear or anxiety, she deposited the Bellasen cross. It was true that everybody knew of it, but nobody knew where it was, and in all probability everybody guessed that it lay at her bankers.

I do not know, for Gimbrell could not tell me, how Davis came to hear of this cross. He heard of it in London, told Gimbrell of it, and offered to take Gimbrell with him, an offer which Gimbrell, much to his credit, refused. It is quite possible that friends of Lady Bellasen's, returning from a visit to her, might have spoken of the cross at a London dinner-table. Servants might have overheard, and might have repeated. Anyhow, Davis knew all about it. He knew in what part of the dining-room the safe stood. He had his plans for getting there, and for crossing over the fell on foot, and returning by a different line.

One night in November Lady Bellasen dined alone, and afterwards busied herself with her history of the Bellasen family. At ten o'clock she called in her two servants, read family prayers to them, and went up to bed. They locked up, and followed her. At a quarter past twelve, Davis, who was an expert burglar, entered through the French windows, which looked out on the garden, and got to work on the safe; he had excellent appliances with him, but the safe gave a good deal of trouble. It was two o'clock before he held the emerald cross in his hands. He had done much hard work, and he was thirsty. The newspapers at the time gave an accurate description of what he drank, and Gimbrell could repeat the whole of it. I am not so sure of myself. I know that it began with a decanter of port. I know that it ended with what was left of the curaçao. I can recall too, that bottled beer figured prominently in the middle of the list, but there were other items which I have forgotten. It took, Gimbrell assures me, a good deal to affect Davis. But in this instance Davis was much affected, and decided to get out of the place at once. During the time that he had been in the house there had been a light fall of snow. He walked out into this, crossed the garden, and made his way up the fell-side. Half-way up, was a tiny plantation, surrounded by a rough stone wall. Here the trees had kept the snow from the ground, and there was plenty of dry bracken. Davis was feeling very tired, and the stiff climb up the fell-side had winded him. He decided to rest for a few minutes, climbed over the wall, and flung himself down on the bracken. In a few moments he was dead asleep, and there he lay for hours, with the clear print of his feet all the way from the plantation to the house, which he had just left. He must, unquestionably, have been much affected.

He woke at daylight, cursed himself for his folly, and determined to get on at once. Looking over the wall of the plantation, he saw the local police, with much volunteer assistance, within a few yards of him. He dropped at once, and they had not seen him. But he knew that they must find him ultimately. At the most it would be a matter of four or five minutes.

He gave himself up quite quietly. "I admit it," he said. "I took the booze. What else could I do? There was the window standing open, lights burning, and liquor on the table. That was at four in the morning, and I'd been out all night. What else could I be expected to do?"

No emerald cross was found on him, and he disclaimed all knowledge of it. He put forward the theory that he had merely followed in the track of a professional burglar, who had taken the cross, and departed, leaving his tools behind him. As far as he was concerned, it was just a case of sudden temptation with him. There was he out all night, cold, hungry, nigh fainting, and he never thought, so help him, that the little drop of sherry wine or what not that he took, would be any great loss to the lady of the house. He took it to save his life. And as for the cross, he was as innocent as an unborn child, my lord.

His theory was not accepted. The different view, which was taken, was based on the fact that Davis had been known to the police as an expert burglar for years, and that he had many previous convictions against him. At this point in Gimbrell's story I thought I might cut the thing short, and asked him where the cross was hidden in the plantation.

"I don't remember saying it was in the plantation," said Gimbrell. "I said it was on 'im when 'e left the 'ouse, and was not on 'im when 'e was took. I don't know where that cross is, and perhaps it's as well I don't. But if a man were to follow Davis as soon as 'e came out, which'll be in a month's time, and to keep on following of 'im, so as not to lose sight of 'im for about a year and a 'alf, I think that chap would be extremely likely to pick up them blooming emeralds."

"Have nothing to do with them, Gimbrell," I said sternly. "Put the thing out of your mind. Those emeralds are stolen property, and you are now an honest man."

I thought the matter over when I got home. Davis must have been drunk when he left the house. His sleep in the plantation would have done him a certain amount of good, and the shock of finding the police within a few yards of him would further have sobered him. He was known to be a man of ready resource. Capture was inevitable, but he could ensure that the cross should not be found on him, and he might even be able to hide it in such a way that he could get it again when he came out of prison. He must, I concluded, have hidden it somewhere or other in the plantation. For that reason, I decided that I would go North for a week's fishing, and told Mrs Pethwick, my housekeeper, to see that my things were packed.

After an uneventful journey, during the greater part of which I slept, I arrived at Arthwaite at nine in the morning. I found a comfortable inn there, and after my bath and my breakfast I went forth. By ten o'clock I had been reminded of the simple fact that anything which occurs to you will probably have occurred to someone else. Not a vestige of that little plantation was left standing. The trees had been cut down and the ground dug. The wall round it had been pulled down and the stones were still there in a big pile. And yet the cross had not been found. I went on to look at the water and to get the requisite permission. I paid for my ticket and went back to the inn. I did not do any fishing that day. I was trying to think out where I was wrong. I must have argued incorrectly with myself, or else the facts from which I had made my deductions were incorrect. Gimbrell's story had been derived partly from Davis, partly from the newspapers, partly from a discharged prisoner, with whom Davis had found means to communicate. The story had not been as full as I might have wished, but I had good reasons for not questioning Gimbrell further. If he had the least suspicion of me, my influence with him for good would be gone forever. Gimbrell might have made some important omission; his memory might have played a trick with him. I thought it at any rate worthwhile to get the newspaper reports of the case. While I waited for these I had a fair day's sport on the river and some talk with my landlord, a round-faced, simple-looking man, who was something of a sportsman, and a good deal more of a poacher. He told me about the plantation. A local landowner, named Harrison, had had it cleared for Lady Bellasen, and the whole work had been done under her inspection. It was reported locally that Harrison, a new arrival, would much like to marry Lady Bellasen, and my landlord hinted that her ladyship was far too proud of the name ever to change it.

The newspapers gave me some additional information. It was a maid-servant who discovered the burglary at half-past six. She immediately rushed upstairs and gave the alarm, and then went back to the kitchen and cried bitterly. No suspicion of any kind attached to her, and I found that she was still in Lady Bellasen's service. On one point the newspapers corrected Gimbrell. She did not dine alone on the night of the burglary. Her brother, Mr Arthur Crowe, was staying in the house. He it was who went for the police as soon as the burglary was discovered, and he and a couple of labourers were present when Davis was captured.

At first sight it did not seem to be a very important correction, but I determined to take the facts as I had now got them and see what I could make of them. The cross was not found on the thief, neither, obviously, had it been hidden in the plantation. Therefore it must have been disposed of at some point between the house and the plantation. I remembered that Davis had suggested that Gimbrell should join him in the job. Failing Gimbrell, could he have had some other confederate, and handed the cross to him? This I could reject at once. There would have been two tracks in the snow instead of one, and the confederate would have realised that Davis was drunk, and would have looked after him better. He certainly would not have allowed him to drop asleep in the plantation. It was far more likely, seeing Davis's condition, that he had dropped it on the way. I had to ask myself when it would have been dropped. It might have been done just as he left the house when he was slipping it into his pocket. It would be a probable piece of drunken clumsiness to miss the pocket, and the cross would make no sound falling on the soft snow. Or it might have been dropped when he was getting over the stile on the way to the plantation. I rejected the latter supposition on the ground that in that case it would certainly have been found. If it was dropped in the garden at a few paces from the house, who would have been the first to see it? Not the servant, for it was admitted that she gave the alarm at once and had never left the house at all. But Mr Arthur Crowe might very likely have found it on his way to the police-station. He might have slipped it in his pocket or, more probably, hidden it somewhere in the garden, where he could easily find it again. So far it seemed probable that if I wanted the Bellasen cross I should have to go to Mr Arthur Crowe for it. Against this probability I had to set the fact that he was a prosperous Plymouth tradesman, and the light of a Dissenting Chapel. He would be quite unable to deal with the emeralds in any way. If he attempted it, he would be detected at once. Briefly, it looked as if the only man who could have taken the cross had no motive whatever for taking it.

While I was in this state of perplexity a little bit of luck came my way. My landlord said to me, "I suppose, sir, you don't know anyone who wants to sell a King Charles spaniel? It would have to be a good pedigree dog. Lady Bellasen is enquiring for one."

"That's a funny thing," I said, "I've got two of them—beauties—and one is all I want. I'll have the other sent down here, and you shall take it to her ladyship."

It cannot be necessary to say that I had no King Charles spaniel at all. But it was perfectly easy to buy one in London, and have it sent down, and I did not wish to neglect anything which could bring me into touch at all with Lady Bellasen.

In due course the dog arrived, and, I regret to say, showed remarkably little affection for its master. The landlord took the hateful little beast over to her ladyship, together with a note from myself, stating the price of the dog, and giving a copy of the pedigree. In the evening I received a courteous reply from her ladyship, and a cheque for the very small sum I had asked for the dog. I put the note and the cheque in my letter case. It might become inconvenient for me if the cashing of that cheque could be traced. Also, I could easily imagine events which would make the production of Lady Bellasen's signature extremely useful to me.

I called my landlord in that night after dinner, and laughed with him over the sale of the dog, asking him what commission he expected. He expected nothing. I said that at least he must help me to drink a bottle of the excellent '87 port which lay in his cellars. It was a necessary exception to my rule. He made no objection, and under the gentle action of the port his tongue became very considerably loosed. Before the end of the evening I had the key to my difficulty—the motive which would lead Mr Arthur Crowe to take that cross and stick to it. I had asked if Lady Bellasen's brother often stopped with her. The landlord shook his head. Crowe had been there only twice, in each case for only one night, and in each case, it was the landlord's belief, that Mr Crowe had invited himself. The landlord described him as a tall man, with a beaky nose, with a scar on his left cheek. I was asked to observe that Lady Bellasen had married right above her family. She had not actively quarrelled with any of them, but she did not care to be on intimate terms. It was hinted to me that Mr Arthur Crowe would have been extremely glad to have trotted her ladyship, his sister, all over Plymouth, and to have impressed his Dissenting friends. They had words about it on the night the cross was stolen. My landlord's ostler's daughter was parlourmaid at Lady Bellasen's, and was waiting at the table that night. That was how my landlord knew. Mr Arthur Crowe had lost his temper and left the house, not returning until prayers were over. That had been his last visit, and no letters had been received from him since. Phrases that he had used were quoted to me. "Your own flesh and blood's not good enough for you now." "All right, I know when I'm not wanted." "Your pride will have a fall one of these days."

There, then, was the motive. The Bellasen cross was the very symbol of the Bellasen pride. Nothing could affect her more than the loss of it. I could imagine him picking it up from the snow, turning back to the house to shout that the cross had not been stolen after all, and then checking himself. His conscience would tell him that he did not intend to reap any profit out of it himself if he kept it. It would be a valuable spiritual lesson to his sister. One day perhaps he would return it. The police theory was still that Davis had hidden the cross. They pointed out that this might have been done at some point beyond the plantation. No suspicion seems to have fallen on Mr Arthur Crowe at all. The only thing that remained for me to do now was to go to Plymouth and steal the cross. As it happened, fate chose to put it in my hands in a simpler and more dramatic way.

I arrived at Plymouth in the afternoon, left my luggage at the station, and went for a stroll to see the town. Presently my eye was caught by a placard on which the name of Mr Arthur Crowe figured largely. The placard stood in the ground of a Dissenting Chapel, then in process of building, and announced that the foundation-stone would be laid by Mr Arthur Crowe on Thursday, the 17th, at three o'clock. As I stood reading the notice, two men who had been talking to the workmen left the chapel. One of them was a short man with an earnest eye and a grey chin-beard. The other was obviously Mr Arthur Crowe. The beaky nose and the scar on the cheek gave him away to me. Neither of the men noticed me, and they walked away together. I walked after them. Mr Crowe had looked to me very ill and very worried. Some point of difference had arisen between Mr Crowe and his friend, and both of them had raised their voices. I followed closely behind them.

"I tell you again," said Mr Crowe, "that I must go up. It is not business which I could leave to anybody else. I shall leave Plymouth by the 8.30 tomorrow morning, and I shall be in London by two; returning the same night, I shall be back in Plymouth, with plenty of time for a good rest, before the ceremony at three o'clock."

"I don't like it," said the little man. "Your health's not good and you're not fit for it. If you go travelling practically all day and all night you'll have a breakdown. And then what are we to do at the laying of the foundation-stone? You're a public man,

Mr Crowe, and it's your duty on a great occasion like this, to nurse yourself in the public interest."

"You are very kind and you mean well," said Mr Crowe, "but I cannot help it. Unless I get through this business in London my mind will not be easy. I doubt if I should be able to go through the ceremony at all. Once the business is over I shall be a new man."

I had heard all I wanted to hear. Mr Crowe was about to deliver himself into my hands. I need hardly say that I travelled up to London next morning in the train with him. I travel first-class always. He, with a laudable love of economy, went third. His figure was rather remarkable, and I had no trouble in finding him again at Paddington Station, from whence he travelled by the underground to Baker Street. So did I. On the platform at Baker Street he was fumbling with a cloak-room ticket which he drew with extreme care from his pocket-book. I went up to the street outside the station and waited. Presently Mr Crowe appeared, carrying a black morocco hand-bag, stamped in gold with his initials. He hailed a four-wheeler.

As the cab drove up I touched him on the arm. "You'll excuse me," I said, "but you are Mr Arthur Crowe, I think."

He turned green and jumped. His nerves were not in a good state. "I am not," he said. "You are mistaken. I don't know you."

I handed him a card, which described me, incorrectly, as Mr Edward Gilroy, private enquiry agent.

"You are Mr Arthur Crowe," I said. "I am here from your sister, Lady Bellasen. Her ladyship is anxious to avoid any scandal, and my instructions are that you are not to be arrested unless you make it inevitable. If you deny that you are Mr Arthur Crowe, you will make it inevitable."

He tried to bluster a little. "Suppose I am? At any rate, you are not a police officer."

"I am not pretending to be. I shall have no trouble in finding a police officer if one is required." I took care to raise my voice on the compromising sentences. "I know perfectly well what you have in that bag. I have been waiting here for you for days. Unless—"

"Stop!" said Mr Arthur Crowe. "Let us talk this over quietly. Do you mind getting into my cab with me? I assure you that I can explain everything."

"Yes," I said, "I'll get into the cab with you." I then turned to the cabman, and said, "Drive to Euston."

"I wasn't going to Euston," Mr Crowe began.

"I know you were not. But you are now. Now, then," I continued, after the cab had started, "Lady Bellasen is prepared on conditions to consider that you took this cross—"

"What cross? What do you mean?"

"If you talk like a child, Mr Crowe, you'll make me angry, and that will not be to your interest. Open the bag which you are nursing so carefully. If the Bellasen cross is not in it, I will apologise and subscribe five hundred pounds to any charity you may name."

He dropped back in his seat, beaten. "All right," he said, "go on."

"Lady Bellasen is prepared, conditionally, to treat this not as a theft, but as a bit of joke on your part. She is prepared to believe that you would have made restitution in any case. When she put the matter in my hands and I discovered that it was you who had taken the cross, this was the course which I advised."

"How did you discover it?"

"That is my special business. You see that I have discovered it."

"I should have restored the cross in any case. Whether you believe it or not, that cross would have been sent off to my sister in a registered parcel this very day."

I fully believed him. "You will excuse me," I said, "if I do not attach much importance to that. In any case her ladyship would not dream of allowing anything so valuable to be risked in the post. My instructions are that you are to hand the cross to me personally, and that I am then to take the next train north from Euston, and deliver it myself to her ladyship."

He made a last effort. "Look here," he said, "supposing I do some of the talking. Why should I hand this to you? How do I know you are acting *bonâfide*?"

"I am beginning to lose patience with you," I said. "Unless you can fulfil her ladyship's condition she will be compelled to take another view of the matter, and we are not proposing to compound a felony." I drew my note-book from my pocket. "You know her ladyship's writing?" I said. "Look at the signature to that letter and to this cheque. Why, if you like, you are perfectly welcome to come back with me and see me yourself, deliver the cross to her ladyship." This was a perfectly safe proposal. On the following afternoon at three I knew that he had an appointment in Plymouth, which he could not miss. But as he did not know that I knew this, he was somewhat impressed.

"I'll tell you what I'll do," he said, as our cab drew up. "I'll see you take your ticket for Arthwaite and telegraph to her ladyship. When you have got into the train I will hand you the cross."

I had no objection. I let him write the telegram himself, and sign it Gilroy. Lady Bellasen only knew me under my own name. The price of a first-class ticket to Arthwaite was no great consideration to a man who had just acquired the Bellasen cross. The train stopped at Willesden, and I got out there, suppressed my Arthwaite ticket, and paid. From Willesden I took a cab back to my house in Bloomsbury, and spent a pleasant evening removing the emeralds from their setting. The metal-work was so beautiful that it really seemed quite a pity to break it up. The emeralds have been disposed of very gradually by me as occasions presented themselves. In fact, some few still remain in my possession.

I felt distinctly pleased with myself over this piece of work, and after the stones had been removed from their setting and safely put away, I rang my bell, and had the brandy brought me. It was an occasion for it.

IX

NUMBERED NOTES

In the course of my work in the East End I have seen a great deal of the misery and vice which result from begging and gambling. I remember on one occasion a poor clerk in whom I was interested being ruined in that way. It began with his taking a few shillings to put on a certainty, with the intention of replacing them as soon as the race was over and he had got his money. The certainty broke down and he was driven to take more money, and more again, always in the hope that he would be able to win enough to replace everything, and with the firm resolve that if this took place he would never bet again. He was discovered, and the law took its usual course. I said then what I repeat now—that it was not so much that poor clerk as the bookmakers who made a profit out of him that ought to have been punished.

Sometime later I had an opportunity myself of punishing the bookmaker. It was a case in which I had to make an exception to my general rule. My general rule, to which I have already alluded, is never to touch numbered notes, but it would have been pedantic for me to have followed it in this case.

At a quarter to two one afternoon I entered an old-fashioned eating-house in the neighbourhood of Victoria Station. I had never been there before—I rather like to go to places where

I have never been before. It seemed to be a house after my own taste, clean, comfortable, wholesome. Welsh mutton and good port would, I felt, be procurable there. I walked into one of the empty boxes and looked over into the next. A big man in a heavy frieze overcoat sat there with his back to me. By his side was a pile of notes, and he was laboriously entering the numbers of them with a stumpy pencil in his pocket-book. I noticed that the notes were in different stages of cleanliness or the reverse, and had not been folded uniformly. The numbers were not consecutive. The man put the notes into a leather satchel which fastened with a spring lock and shut the pocket-book. As he did this I slipped out of the box in which I was and entered his. There I sat down and picked up the bill of fare. I had not at the moment determined to do anything, but there was a good deal of money within a few yards of me, and it was worthwhile to think about it.

As I read the bill of fare I watched my man. He deposited the satchel by his side, and put the pocket-book in the inside pocket of his heavy overcoat, of which he now proceeded to divest himself. There were hat pegs at his end of the box, and he hung his coat on one of them. "Will you oblige me, sir?" I asked, as I handed him my own coat. He took it and hung it on the next peg without a word, and dropped heavily into his seat again. He was clearly a sulky, gruff, contemptuous, powerful beast. He did not mean to talk to me or anybody else more than could be avoided. His order to the waiter was "Chopanboiled."

"Yes, sir," said the waiter. "Anything to drink?"

The big man stared before him with eyes that were just a little fishy, as if he had not heard. After a few seconds of reflection he growled an abbreviated order for sixpenny-worth of a particular brand of whisky, which I cannot advertise by naming here. He was not drunk, not in the least drunk. All the same, he had been drinking.

I gave the waiter my order and asked him to bring me a newspaper. He brought me a morning paper.

"Funny thing," I said, "that you can never get an evening paper in this neighbourhood before three in the afternoon." It was to the waiter that I said this. The best way, I felt, to make my friend with the bank-notes talk, was not to talk to him. He tumbled into my little trap at once. "What, sir?" he said. "Why there's a boy selling them outside the door now, and any amount more of them down the street."

"You will excuse me, sir," I said, "but I'm afraid I must contradict you. I've just come in and I say there was no boy."

"You mean you didn't see him. He's there right enough, that's his pitch."

"Is it? Well, I can see without spectacles. I wouldn't mind making a small bet that you can't go out and bring an evening paper back with you inside of three minutes."

"Would you?" he said grimly. "If you like to have a sovereign on it, I'm your man."

I hesitated. "A sovereign is rather more than I intended," I said.

"I thought it would be," said my friend contemptuously.

"All right, then," I said, very much as if I were losing my temper. I fumbled in my pocket, and slapped my sovereign down on the table. "There you are," I said. "If you can show as much, it's a bet."

He pulled a loose handful of gold out of his trouser pocket. "That do for you?" he said. He snatched up his hat and the satchel containing his notes. "Now then," he said, "you can take your time by the clock over there."

The moment he had gone I made the interesting discovery that I had left my handkerchief in the breast-pocket of my overcoat. While my left hand, which was in view of the waiter at the other end of the room, was getting my handkerchief out of that pocket, my right hand was removing the pocket-book from the lower pocket of my friend's overcoat This hand was entirely screened by the partition. Then I had to move pretty quickly. I tore out the page which contained the numbers of the notes, shut the pocket-book again, and put it back in the same place. I was seated at my own end of the box, watching the clock intently, when he entered—triumphant of course, and with an evening paper in his hand.

"Well, you surprise me," I said. "I could have sworn there was no boy there when I came in. However, it can't be helped. A bet's a bet. Perhaps I'll make another one with you before we've finished."

"I've no objection," said the big man, as he pocketed my sovereign, "supposing that it's anything I care to bet on. I'll give you a fair chance anyhow."

His contempt was obvious. He was a sharp man, and had found that there were many fools in the world. Given any signs of acuteness on my part, he would have been on his guard at once. As it was, he classed me at once as the usual ass, and felt that he could play with me as he liked, and that I might be worth another sovereign or two to him. It was perhaps with a prospective view to this sovereign or two that he handed me the evening paper.

"There you are, sir. It's yours—or ought to be. I'm sure you paid enough for it, and paid up like a sportsman, I'll say that for you."

The purport of his little bit of flattery did not escape me, but I smiled with sufficient fatuousness. All the time I was thinking hard. I had got the numbers of the notes, and he had no other record of them. To get the notes themselves seemed likely to be a more difficult business. I rather like the use of drugs on these occasions, and I had what I wanted in my pocket. But to get it out, and to administer it without detection seemed to me pretty well impossible. If I had made a second bet with him which involved his leaving the room, it is quite possible that he would have become suspicious. I could not risk that.

"Seems you're a teetotaller," he said, glancing at the soda-water that I was drinking. "Quiright. Very good thing. I am pretty nigh a teetotaller myself. Rare thing for me to indulge. Waiter, take this damn glass back, and have another sixpenn'orth put in it."

I am not a teetotaller. I drink when I wish to get drunk, but not otherwise. It seemed to me that this was an occasion on which, whether I won or lost, intoxication would be reasonable, and there was no objection to my taking the first step towards it now.

"Teetotaller?" I said. "Not a bit of it. I'm simply a moderate man, same as yourself. I wasn't taking anything with my lunch, because I meant to try a little port afterwards, and I'll ask you to join me."

"Now you're talking like a sensible man. I'll join you with pleasure. I'll do more for you than that. Do you know this house?"

"Never been here before."

"Well, I know the people here and they know me, and I can tell you what's the best thing to order, and it's not the most expensive port on the list either."

I said that I should be very glad to leave it to him, and the waiter was called. The waiter looked pityingly at me, as at a pigeon, who has fallen in with a hawk. My friend was undoubtedly well known there.

The wine was brought. "Thash where I have the advantage of you," he said. "I'm a licensed victualler myself. Orram's my name—very well-known name. You ask about Mr James Orram anywhere in Fulham, they'll tell you." He winked sagaciously, and finished his first glass. "Goosstuff," he observed.

"Yes," I said, "very good port indeed." The drug that I use can be procured, if you know how to get it, in tabloid form.

As I spoke I unscrewed the top of the phial in my waistcoat pocket. Presently I had one tabloid out. Chance might put something in my way, or I might manage to get the tabloid into the decanter when there were only two glasses left. It would be easy enough for me to have an accident with my own glass.

Chance did put something in my way, but it was something quite different. I had noticed that the room was getting very dark, and now the waiter came forward and lit the gas above us. "A regular pea-souper outside, sir," he said to Orram, in a familiar way. "Come up pretty sudden too."

"Yes," I said, "it was pretty thickish in the city this morning."

"You a city man?" asked Orram.

"Yes," I said, "in the provision business. Burnside's my name. We've had some crates gone wrong, that's how it was I came to Victoria. I shan't go back to work if the weather stops like this."

"Quiright," said Orram enthusiastically. "Who wants work? I don't want to work. Let's go to a music hall."

"Right you are!" I said. "And perhaps we'll have a bit of dinner together afterwards. I don't care if I do make a day of it, for once in a way. Come along. Waiter, call a four-wheeler."

"Make it a 'ansom," said Orram. "I like a 'ansom myself."

"So do I," I said, "but not in this weather. We should want the glass down, and you can't smoke in a hansom with the glass down. I've got some cigars here that I'm not ashamed of."

Orram took one, lit it, and saw that it was good. "You're a goosort," he said appreciatively.

The waiter brought our bills, and told us that the four-wheeler was waiting at the door. Orram paid his bill and corrected a mistake of the waiter's in the change. He picked up his satchel, flung his overcoat over his arm, and walked out straight. It was only in his speech that one detected that he had been drinking too much. By this time my little plan, which was simplicity itself, was quite formed.

When we had got into the cab and were crawling slowly eastward, I reminded my friend that he had promised to give me a chance to win my money back.

"Very well," he said, "what are you grumbling at? It's for you to speak, isn't it? As soon as there's anything you fancy, you can mention it. I'm a man of my word. It would take a blankly lot more than a sovereign to break me. Make it a fiver if you like. Can't we get this blankly funeral to go a bit quicker? The show will be done before we get there."

"The roads are pretty slippery," I said, "and it's too dark to drive fast anyhow. Look here, suppose we have a bet as to which of us is the first to see a horse down. You look out of one window and I'll look out of the other."

"Give me choice of windows?" he asked cunningly.

"Certainly," I said, with apparent simplicity.

"Right," said Orram. "Change over then. I'll take the off side and leave you the near. If you do see a horse down, it'll have to be on the pavement."

"I don't know about that," I said. "I may spot one down a side street or in front or behind. I'll chance my fiver on it anyhow."

I leaned right out of the window.

"All right, my son," said Mr Orram, "two can play at that game." He, in his turn, leaned right out of the window. While he was in this position I picked up his satchel, opened the door of the cab, and under cover from a passing 'bus, jumped out.

That was quite a useful 'bus. I slipped round to the far side of it, by which means I was screened from the driver of the four-wheeler. At the same time I asked myself what a man in my circumstances would naturally do. I decided that he would go back, so that the distance between himself and the four-wheeler might be increased as rapidly as possible. This being so, I took the exactly opposite course. I walked leisurely along on the pavement in the same direction that the four-wheeler was going. For the moment it was blocked, and I easily got ahead of it. I was about twenty yards away when I heard the row begin. Probably my friend had looked round to make some remark to me, and had discovered my absence, and the still more painful absence of his satchel. So far as I could tell, a vigorous search was being made in the wrong direction. I turned down Dover Street, and there, under the friendly veil of the fog, I cut open the satchel and took out the notes. I put the notes in my pocket, and dropped the satchel. On reaching home, I examined the notes and rejected two or three of them, owing to marks on their back, which I did not like. These I burnt, and I hope the Bank of England feels grateful to me. The rest I changed at different times, and the net result was eighty-five pounds. It was a nice little morning's work. It was a pleasant reflection also for me that this sharp, gambling sportsman would find himself outwitted by the simpleton whom he had despised, and that he would, if anything, be even more angry with himself than with me.

The story had a sequel about six months later. I was driving in a hansom in Tottenham Court Road, and another hansom met us going in the opposite direction. In the other hansom sat Mr Orram. He recognised me, leaned forward and shook his fist. I glared stonily at him. I flatter myself that there was not one sign of comprehension or recognition in my face. I saw his hand shoot up to the trap in the roof, and I knew that he would have his cab turned round and would follow me. My horse was not a very good one, and I knew the constable on the pavement a few yards ahead. I stopped my cab, got out as if to enter a shop, suddenly recognised the constable, and stopped for a moment's chat with him. Up drove Mr Orram, white and furious. He tumbled out of his cab, before it had stopped, and rushed up to me.

"Now then, by God! I've got you!" he shouted.

The constable paid attention. I smiled.

"What's the matter, my good man?" I asked. Disguise of face was impossible, but disguise of manner was very easy. I was no longer the vacuous mug that I had pretended to be when he saw me before. I was grave, sensible and unperturbed. Mr Orram observed that I was the—something unprintable who had robbed him. I turned to the policeman.

"I have never seen this man in my life before," I said. "You can tell him who I am. Possibly he's made some mistake."

"Made a pretty big 'un!" said my friend the policeman, and began to talk to Orram in a distinctly unsympathetic manner, telling him to go away and not to make a fool of himself.

Unfortunately, Mr Orram had been drinking. He was also perfectly certain that he had got the right man, and furious that his word was doubted. Finally, he so far forgot himself as to attempt to push the policeman out of the way in order to get at me. Now, in England policemen may not be pushed.

He was let off rather lightly. There was no doubt he had been robbed some time before, and that he had believed that he had secured the thief. This did not justify him in the course he had taken, especially as the policeman had been able to point out to him the absurdity of the blunder. I fancy Orram must himself have been convinced in the end that it was a blunder, for I met him once since, and, after careful inspection, he went on his way without a word.

X

IMPERSONATION

When I walk in a crowded London street my eyes are open and my ears are quick to hear. The man who seeks his opportunities sooner or later finds them. I should imagine that every day in Oxford Street and Regent Street alone chances representing a million of money are thrown away because people cannot see their opportunities. It is not scrupulousness that stops them, it is stupidity. It has always been a pleasure to me to feel that if I were put down in the middle of London without one acquaintance in the place and without one penny in my pocket, I should always be able to make enough to pay for my board and lodging. I should probably make very much more than that.

I was walking in Oxford Street at eleven o'clock one morning in the height of the season when a little old lady, quietly and expensively dressed, crossed the pavement from a book shop to her carriage. The carriage was a one-horse brougham, and one of the shop assistants opened the door for her. She directed him to tell the coachman to drive to Saronel's in Bond Street. The old lady had beautiful white hair. She carried in her hand a religious magazine that she had probably purchased in the shop. All these and other points I noted carefully, and principally among the other points I noted a certain strangeness in her appearance. Quiet though she was in her manner the possibility of some mental disorder occurred to me. I think it was the restless look in her eyes which gave me the idea.

When a woman who, if appearances may be trusted, may be insane, drives to the principal Bond Street jeweller's shop, it is worth while for a sane man, of my way of thinking, to follow. There may be nothing in it, but in these matters one must have patience. What was likely to be in it, and how I was to get at it, never even occurred to me at this juncture. Things had not developed far enough. All the same I took the next hansom, and told the man to drive to Taverner's. Traverner's, you will remember, is the big boot shop next to Saronel's.

My cab pulled up just behind the brougham, which was waiting for the old lady outside Saronel's. What was I to do next? The old lady's coachman looked very sleepy. I could have entered the brougham without making enough noise to attract his attention. When the old lady entered the carriage one strong hand over her mouth would keep her quiet until a few threats saved the necessity for any further violence. The idea had some points about it, but was quite unpractical. She would see me as soon as the door was opened, and she would not enter the brougham. If she did, and the rest of my plan was carried out, and I possessed myself of anything that she had purchased at Saronel's, I had still to find some way of escaping safely with my prize. Also it was quite possible, that the old lady was merely having her watch regulated or buying a three-and-sixpenny stamp box for a wedding present.

No, it was clearly better to see a little more what was happening before taking any action whatever. I walked into Saronel's and took a seat at the counter on the other side of the shop, and at some distance from the old lady. A mirror showed me everything that she did. I told the assistant that I wanted some interesting specimens of Labradorite, preferably in the form of carved heads mounted as rings or scarf pins. The order, as I had expected, took a couple of minutes to execute, and during that time I watched the old lady.

She sat upright and impassive, while two assistants showed her one thing after another. The counter in front of her was cumbered with trays and cases. Occasionally she shook her head. She was apparently hard to please.

However, by the time that the man who was waiting on me had discovered that they had not the exact thing that I wanted in stock, and that I would not trouble them to procure it for me, and that I would not buy anything else instead, the old lady had made her choice. It was a pearl necklace of great beauty and, I judged, of great value.

"No," she said to one of the assistants in rather a peevish voice, "you needn't send anybody with it at all. I shall be passing again this afternoon, and I will then have the cheque for you. You will see that the necklace is packed up ready for me."

She gave them her card, and wrote the name of her bankers, to whom they were to refer, upon it. Then she got up from her chair and dropped her pencil.

The assistant who had come round to open the door for her stooped to pick it up.

She had just three moments in which she was perfectly safe, and she used these three moments well. She was as quick as light, and as unperturbed as a statue. There was no trace of hurry, no sign of embarrassment.

I followed her out, and, on the pavement touched her gently on the arm and raised my hat.

"You would save yourself the unpleasantness of a public disturbance, Lady Mardon," I said, "if you would act as if you knew me. I am from Scotland Yard, and I have had you under observation for a long time past. I was watching you in Saronel's just now, and I saw everything that happened."

She was frightened, but she smiled.

"You are really making some mistake," she said. "The only thing that happened in Saronel's was that I ordered a pearl necklace."

"In that case," I said, "perhaps you would oblige me by putting on your other glove. It is of no use to talk to me in that way, you see. I not only saw you take the diamond star, but I have now shown you that I know where you are hiding it at this moment."

"Don't take me to the police station," she said. "I didn't know what I was doing. I take drugs. I can explain everything to you."

"I am afraid," I said, "that I must carry out my duty. As you know, this is not the first time by a long way."

"I have never been inside Saronel's in my life before."

"I can quite believe that you would not go to the same establishment twice."

"Listen," she said eagerly. "I have got every single thing that I took. They are all at my house. I can show them to you if you like. If you will come with me in my carriage, I will hand them over to you at once."

"Very well," I said, "it is quite immaterial to me. But I will come with you and collect the stolen property first; you will have to come on to the station with me afterwards."

This woman, like many women thieves, was extremely simple and ignorant. It was clear to me now that I ran not the slightest risk of discovery by her. We entered her brougham. All the way to South Kensington, where her house was, she sat with her head in her hands, hiding her face, not speaking a word, occasionally trembling violently.

The situation was an extremely promising one. All that she had stolen would be handed over to me. In addition I felt that the detective inspector should have some *solatium* for the remorse that he would feel at neglecting his duty and allowing this criminal to go scot-free. I had no intention of proposing anything of the kind myself: that would be certain to come from her.

I guessed the rent of her house at £350 per annum. It was most luxuriously furnished, and her servants were good, expensive servants. Clearly she had no necessity to steal at all. It was a bad case. I said as much when we were seated in the library together. She had regained her composure now.

"I am not going to discuss with you," she said, "whether it is a bad case or not. I am alone in the world, and I am accustomed to look after myself. I have foreseen for some time past the extreme probability that this would happen, and I have made ready for it. You must have noticed how little surprised I was when you arrested me. Now I've got just two things to say to you. The first is that you can take me to the police station if you like, but that you will never get me there alive. The second thing I will put in quite a plain and simple way. Every man has his price. What is yours?"

"Your threat of committing suicide, Lady Mardon, has but one effect upon me—to make it impossible for you to carry it out. I had hoped to spare you the handcuffs, but I see that I shall have to use them. You will have no chance whatever of committing suicide. Your attempt to bribe me will, I am afraid, make the case seem all the blacker against you. Now, please, if you will show me the rest of the property that you have stolen, that will tell to some extent in your favour, and then we can be getting on."

"Listen," she said. "You are a detective, an inspector, I suppose, or something of that kind. Are you a man as well?"

"What is the good of wasting time like this?" I said impatiently.

"I am going to tell you my story as briefly as possible. I don't want money, and have never wanted it. I have had great sufferings—bereavements that have left me alone in the world. I could not sleep when I had acute neuralgia. You know what that leads to; you know what this is?" She took up a little leather case from the table, and opened it

I nodded. "Yes," I said, "hypodermic syringe."

"Well, then, if you are a man as well as a police officer, it will be enough for you that justice is done. It is not detectives and magistrates that I want, it is doctors and nurses. Sometimes in a shop or in Society I see something sparkle in a particular way. It is impossible for me to describe it. When that happens, I have no more control over myself. I have to take the thing that sparkles like that. After I have got it, I do not want it. I put it away where I cannot see. I am wretched about it, and fly to the morphia again. I will show you all that I have taken."

She unlocked and opened a drawer in the escritoire. It contained twenty packets. Each one bore an address and a date. It was a marvel of method—of insane orderliness.

"There," she said, "you can take them all, please, and send them back. As long as these people recover their property they won't want to punish a poor old half-mad woman. Nor will you if you are a man at all."

I appeared to hesitate. "I hardly know what to say," I said. "If I had any choice in the matter I should undoubtedly do as you wish. I am not inhuman, and I admit that the story that you have told me has made some effect upon me. But look at the risk that I run if I do not do my duty. I may very possibly be discovered, and may lose my employment."

"How can you be discovered? You who are so clever in tracking others can find ways to hide your own actions. But I will pay you for the risk you run. I will pay you a hundred pounds. You shall return the stolen property yourself, and I promise you that I will put myself in the hands of a good doctor this afternoon. You needn't be afraid. I shall never take anything again. I've had my lesson."

I walked up and down the room. I was sorry to appear grasping, and I told her so, but I reminded her that I was risking a salary of four hundred pounds a year on account of her, and that I might possibly find myself in prison as well. If she would insure me half a year's salary, I should, if dismissed, at any rate have the time to look about me and find some other employment. She saw the point of my arguments, and said that she would write me a cheque for two hundred pounds.

"No," I said, "that will not do. Cheques can be traced and notes can be traced; sovereigns cannot. I must have a cab to take away these parcels with me, and I will drive you to your bank. When you have handed over to me the two hundred sovereigns that you will obtain there, I will let you return again to your own house, and after that you will never hear from me or see me again."

I fastened the parcels together in one package. A four-wheeler was called, and we started off.

Really that woman was quaint beyond words. She sank back in the cab with a sigh of relief.

"Honestly," she said, "I am glad this has happened. It had to happen one day. I always knew it. I might have fallen into the hands of a man with no humanity at all, a mere automaton carrying out prescribed duties regardless of everything else. It will be a turning point in my life too. I have not liked to recognise that I was ill. Anything wrong with one's mind or one's control over one's self always seems so disgraceful. But I shall recognise it now. Yes, today I shall put myself in the hands of the best specialist that I can find." She tapped the parcel significantly. "Nothing of this kind any more. Never again!"

I asked her about the transaction with the pearl necklace.

"Oh, that is quite all right," she said. "I shall certainly go back to Saronel's and pay for it as I said I would. It is a wedding present to a near relation of mine."

"You will not be afraid that they will have missed the diamond star?"

"Of course they will have missed it. But they will never dream that I took it. A lady who can afford to buy a pearl necklace for eight hundred pounds, would not steal a little diamond star worth perhaps twenty-five. At any rate, that will be their argument."

There were certainly strange gleams of shrewdness about her. She brought me the money from the bank, and as we drove away I counted it and found it correct. I stowed it away in different pockets—two hundred sovereigns take up rather more space than most people suppose—tucked the big parcel under my arm, stopped the cab and got out. I walked for a few hundred yards, and then took another cab home.

Frankly, the parcel was a great disappointment. There was a great deal of silver rubbish in it. I suppose that a beam of light had fallen on it and made it sparkle, and given it that fascination that she described. There were three or four good rings, all set with sapphires, but nothing else of importance.

I took most of the stuff out with me next day on my motor-car, stopped in a lonely country road, and threw them over the hedge. It was not the kind of stuff that I could deal with, and it was dangerous to keep it.

Three days later Lady Mardon, who of course had not reformed—that kind never does reform—was caught by a real detective—one of those callous automata to which she had referred. She told a singularly wild story to the police, but they took very little notice of it. The scandal in high life helped to fill the newspapers for a few days, and then, on the medical evidence, she was acquitted.

Speaking calmly and judicially, I think that this was perhaps the most dastardly theft I ever committed.

XI

THE CHANGE

About this time, under circumstances of no particular interest, I secured for myself two days' takings of the Stafford Restaurant in Regent Street and the weeks' wages of the Estville Drug Factory in Northampton. I was also present at a large and fashionable bazaar in South Kensington, and after I had gone it was found that the money received for admission at the doors had gone also. I could not approve of the object of the bazaar—the restoration of a church. It is not so much the churches as the congregations that it is necessary to restore. At the same time, I had no intention of taking this money when I went to the bazaar. I went there, because at such gatherings I frequently pick up information which is afterwards useful. I took the money because the opportunity arose. It has often happened that opportunity has done more for me than the most elaborate and well-matured plan; but one must have great rapidity of mind to see the chance and to avail one's self of it. As I have said, these little incidents, though profitable and therefore welcome, were too commonplace for detailed record.

Rather more interesting was the case of the bank messenger. I first came upon it two years before in the morning papers. The messenger, James Gladden by name, was a man of great experience, perfect probity, and remarkable physique. No ordinary man would have cared to tackle him, at any rate with Nature's weapons. He had been sent to the office of a solicitor in Westminster, to receive a large sum in gold and notes, with which he was to return to the city. He put the money in his bag, which was chained and locked in the usual way, and it was suggested to him that he should take a cab back. Gladden said that he considered the railway safer, quicker, and cheaper; besides he had taken a return ticket. He entered an empty second-class compartment at Westminster Bridge. At the Temple Station a lady opened the door of the carriage, and found Gladden lying senseless on the floor; his bag with the chain attached to it had vanished. Gladden's story, when he recovered consciousness, was plain and simple enough. The train had been stopped outside Charing Cross Station, and Gladden had put his head out of the window to see if he could make out the reason for the stop. As he drew his head back again, it was struck violently from behind and he fell senseless. He never saw his assailant, who must either have been concealed under the seat or have entered the carriage from the other side while Gladden was looking out of the window. Naturally, Gladden was closely questioned and watched, but he was never really suspected. He was, indeed, quite guiltless in the matter, and I cannot even think that he was indiscreet. The bank took the same view, and still employs him.

The affair created a good deal of sensation at the time. One man was arrested on suspicion, but it was clear that he had nothing to do with this particular crime, and he was released. The numbers of the notes had, of course, been taken, and these numbers were published and the notes were stopped. Weeks passed and no attempt was made to present the notes, and public interest in the matter lapsed. The thief, whoever he was, might have got clear away at Charing Cross before the theft was discovered.

The success of the detective depends in stories on his remarkable acumen and his still more remarkable luck. I have analysed some of these stories and found always some thousand-to-one chance favouring the detective. In real life the detective depends less on his own personal brilliance or on thousand-to-one chances than on a well-managed organisation, placing unusual sources of information at his disposal. In the case of the bank messenger Scotland Yard had nothing to go upon, no point from which to start, and was completely at fault. The detectives could put their hands easily on a number of known men who were quite likely to commit a crime of this kind, but there was no evidence to connect any one of them with it.

I also had my sources of information. I have worked long among the criminal classes, and have laboured hard and not without success at the reformation of some of these poor fellows. But it has never been as a servant of the police that I have worked; if the slightest suspicion of "narking" had ever fallen upon me my work would have been ruined. I depend absolutely on their trust and confidence in me. I am not seeking to bring them to human justice but to a mercy more than human. Yes, I can imagine the scorn on my reader's face, the words of contempt that he will hiss at me. Believe me, they are unfair. I have been a man of double life, but each side has been sincere and genuine. I may go further than that, and say that, on the whole, the better side is the more potent, and will last the longer. If you have the patience to read on, you will see what reason I have to say this.

As I have said, I had my sources of information. I talked to one or two men of my acquaintance who had in their time been criminals, and were still likely to hear of any important *coup* in the criminal world. They had no definite information to give me, but one of them, Alfred Gimbrell, had a theory. Gimbrell was a man of low intelligence and the simplest arithmetical problem would have been beyond him; but he showed a certain amount of cunning in criminal matters.

"That were none of us," said Gimbrell decisively. "It were a ammyture what done that, and he were a lucky 'un."

A professional would have had a plan; the assailant clearly had none, for he could not have told that the train would stop just outside Charing Cross, or that, if the train did stop, Gladden would put his head out of the window. A professional would not have taken absurd and unnecessary risks; he would not have changed carriages; he would have committed the robbery just after leaving a station, not when the train was on the point of entering a station and interruption was probable; he would have hit much harder—the injury to Gladden had been very slight—and he would have rolled the senseless body out of sight under the seat.

Such, put in other words, were Gimbrell's arguments, and there was undoubtedly something in them. But a clever criminal is as ready to take advantage of a sudden opportunity as to work on a pre-conceived plan, though he may prefer the plan.

There seemed to be no prospect of my finding out any more than the police had done, and after all detective business has no attractions for me. I carefully memorised the numbers of the missing notes—there were six of £100 and one of £50—in case some unprincipled person might attempt to get me to change any of them. Otherwise, I gave the matter no more attention.

An incident now occurred to recall the whole thing to my memory. Shortly after my profitable little adventure at that fashionable bazaar, I determined to take a short holiday. I had had much work in connection with a series of revivalist meetings, and I felt that I had earned a period of luxurious rest. Also, I could very well afford it; quite apart from the money which I had made in other ways, some speculative investments of mine had turned out remarkably well. Indeed, I was in such a position that I could live in fair comfort for the remainder of my days without resorting to those methods of increasing my income which I had hitherto employed. I thought this over, but without any immediate intention of relinquishing these methods. It was not the fascinating excitement of theft or burglary which mastered me; this it is which has often led criminals of great ability to attempt some impossible *coup* to their undoing. I was influenced in some degree by a desire to make yet more money, and to a still greater degree by fatalism. I saw myself as the winning piece on the board, checkmating time after time the feeble defence of stupid people against relentless and unscrupulous brains, but yet moved by a hand which I was powerless to resist. All that I determined at present was to leave England for a period of rest and enjoyment.

A few weeks later I was in the bureau of my hotel at Nice, making some enquiries, when a woman entered whose appearance made some impression upon me. Her age was perhaps twenty-eight, her figure was slight and graceful. She was beautiful, and at a first glance seemed to me to be unhappy; I looked at her again and judged her to be absolutely desperate. Yet when she addressed the clerk it was with perfect composure. She spoke good and fluent French, but was clearly an Englishwoman.

"I want you to take charge of these," she said, handing over a note-case, stamped in gold with the initials G. E. "Please put them in your safe, and give me a receipt for them."

The clerk took out the notes. There were six of them of £100 and one of £50, and wrote down their numbers. He handed her a receipt, and she passed out. She had dropped her handkerchief in drawing the note-case from her muff. I now dropped my own handkerchief and under cover of it picked up hers as well. I had intended to go over to Monte Carlo that morning, but this promised to be more interesting than the tables. I went for a stroll by myself.

The lady had given the name of Miss Endelwode—the clerk had had some difficulty in spelling it—and the number of her room was 127. The notes were those which had been stolen from Gladden, the bank messenger. I had read the numbers at a glance as the clerk wrote them down. It is quite easy to read upside-down writing with a little practice. On my lonely walk I examined the lady's handkerchief. It was of exquisite quality, perfumed with Russian leather, and bore in one corner the initials E. E.

In the case of a man or, indeed, of most women, my course would have been clear enough. I should have practised some veiled and discreet method of blackmail, and made my holiday expenses, and there the matter would have ended. As it was, my judgment was perhaps somewhat warped by my feelings. For instance, I felt a distinct relief that the initials on the handkerchief were not identical with those on the note-case. On my return to the hotel I wrote the following letter:

"Dear Madam,

Permit me to return to you the handkerchief which you dropped in the bureau this morning. May I at the same time add that the numbers of the notes which you then left with the cashier are of great interest to many people, and that you will be well advised to exercise the greatest care in dealing with them in any way?—I am, madam, your obedient servant, Constantine Dix."

I had this letter sent to her room, and then waited for her to take the next step. She took it after dinner, as I sat in the lounge and sipped my coffee. She came straight up to me, and she no longer looked desperate or even unhappy. But she did look decidedly angry.

"You are Mr Dix, I believe."

"I am."

"An extremely impertinent letter has been left in my room signed with your name."

"I sent a letter to your room, but without any intention of being impertinent. My only intention was to warn you. You are running a very serious risk—unconsciously, no doubt."

She shrugged her pretty shoulders. "I don't understand you in the least. How long would it take you to explain yourself?"

"Two minutes—in any place where I can speak privately."

"I will give you two minutes. Come out into the garden."

I followed her into the garden of the hotel. It was a gorgeous night, full of flowers and fragrance and moonlight.

"As quickly as you can," she said.

"Certainly. I have no means of knowing how these notes came into your possession, but they were stolen two years ago in the underground railway near Charing Cross, from James Gladden, a bank messenger in the employment of Stanniwell & Co., of Lombard Street."

She perceptibly flinched, and hesitated for a moment. "How am I to know that there is a word of truth in this?"

"Send the numbers of the notes to Stanniwell & Co., or to Scotland Yard, or to the Bank of England, and ask for information."

Again there was a perceptible hesitation. "I suppose," she said slowly, "you think that I stole the notes."

"On the contrary, I am quite certain that you did not."

"And what makes you certain?"

"If it is not impertinent to say so, I have seen and observed you. I trust appearances when I observe them myself."

"Why didn't you declare that the notes were stolen when you saw me at the bureau? Why didn't you go to the police at once? Unless, of course, you expected to make more out of it in this way."

I laughed. "Quite a natural idea," I said, "not very complimentary to myself, but quite natural. It leaves me with nothing more to say—besides, my two minutes are up. Good-evening, Miss Endelwode."

Her whole manner changed in a flash. "I'm sorry I said that—I didn't mean it. I will believe that you want to—to help me. Only, if you do, help me a little further. Hear what I've got to say, Do stay." She sat down on a rustic seat beside the path, and I took my place next to her. Away, through the trees, one saw the scattered lights of the hotel, and caught the sound of violins and the deep vibrating note of the cello.

"Perhaps you were mistaken this morning," she said, "when you felt so sure that I was perfectly honest."

"I felt sure that you were naturally and intrinsically honest. Circumstances are very strong, and few—if any—are always perfectly honest."

"I don't mean that I knew definitely these notes were stolen. They came into my possession quite properly; but I did know there was something wrong about them."

"Only," I continued, "this morning you were at your wit's end. You were desperate. You could not see what else to do."

"You're rather wonderful, for that is quite true. Listen, I'll tell you the whole story. About a year and a half ago my uncle died suddenly. I had never been allowed to see him, and a vague impression had been given me that he was a bad lot. My father went up to my uncle's lodgings in London, attended the funeral, and arranged matters generally. My uncle had been a constant source of trouble and expense to my father, and I think my father felt the death rather as a relief than as a sorrow. Certainly, I remember him saying when he came back home after the funeral, that much worse might have happened, and heaven alone knew what calamity we had been spared. A few days later my father had a paralytic stroke, and within a few hours he also was dead, and I was left alone in the world. I am, I believe, the last living Endelwode."

"Your mother?"

"She died when I was a child of eight. My father was a country vicar; the living was small, and he used to say that he was the poorest man in his parish. However, he kept up his insurance premiums, and when everything was settled up I had a thousand pounds absolutely at my disposal. What unending wealth it seemed to me then! I came up to London, first to a hotel and afterwards to lodgings; I visited some distant relatives, and tried to make up my mind what to do with my life."

She paused, almost as if her story were done. I watched her intently. At the mention of these relatives the expression of her face grew hard and bitter.

"Doesn't all this bore you?" she asked. "No? Well, I've not yet told you about the notes, have I? I had brought with me a portmanteau packed with my father's papers. They were mostly sermons, or letters from churchwardens on parish matters, or letters from my uncle asking for a loan. However, I had to go through them before destroying them. On the top of these bundles was a sealed envelope, and inside were the notes in the case with my uncle's initials, just as you saw it today. And—I'm not going to shield myself—there was a pencil memorandum in my father's writing. It was headed 'In the event of my death'—it is queer how often people who have these strokes have some presentiment of coming ill—and then it said, 'Found at 42 Denworth Square. To be returned to their rightful owner when found, and until then to be kept intact.' My uncle's lodgings were at 42 Denworth Square. My father must have found them there on my uncle's death, and must have known that if my uncle had dared to use them to free himself from debt or for some further selfgratification, he would certainly have done so."

"And what have you done," I asked, "to find out who was the rightful owner of this money?"

"Yes," she said slowly, twisting her handkerchief in her hands, "you are right to ask that. By the light of transparent masculine honesty a woman can see how vain and mean she has been."

Transparent masculine honesty—that phrase cut me like a whiplash across the face. Yet so far as she was concerned I was honest.

"Pardon me," I said, "but I have no rights at all in the matter. Whatever you tell me, I shall still believe that you are naturally honest. Whatever you tell me, I shall still be anxious to serve you in any way that you will permit. Tell me as much as you will or as little. If it gives you a moment's pain to speak, I pray you to tell me nothing. My belief in you will still be the same."

Then rather a disconcerting thing happened. Miss Endelwode put her head in her hands and began to cry. It was only for a moment or two. She controlled herself wonderfully.

"I'm sorry I've made a fool of myself. I've been through the most awful strain today—you shall hear about it directly—and I suppose it has rather broken me up. I must tell you everything. You trust me like that—why, I couldn't be happy if I didn't tell you. What did I do to find the owner of the notes? Very little. I hunted the papers for advertisements referring to them and found none. But I myself never advertised. My father would have done so—he had more courage than I in matters of principle—and it was not any desire to keep the notes which stopped me. I had my own thousand pounds, and wanted no more then. It was simply that I was afraid of any enquiry. I suspected that my uncle had not come by these notes honestly, and I imagined our name in all the papers, and myself in the witness-box. I could not face it. Then something happened to turn my mind to other things, and I tell it from no vanity. I have spoken of a visit to some distant relatives. They lived at Hampstead, and I did not find them very sympathetic. There was a girl in the house—she was some far-away cousin of mine—she had canary-coloured hair and a general exuberance, and I took little interest in her. She was engaged to a young man in whom I took even less interest; he was just beautifully and perfectly average. I thought I knew absolutely everything that he would do and say, until one day he suddenly proposed to me. Well, I flayed him alive. At least I did my best."

I laughed. "I have some reason to know that your best in that direction is pretty good, Miss Endelwode."

"Don't!" she said pleadingly. "I know I was horrible at first, when I had only your letter to go by. But I did see afterwards that I had made a mistake—no, it was not only what you said—I also judge a good deal by appearances. Yes, I was telling you about that young man. I suppose some brilliant idea of sex-revenge struck him. At any rate he jilted the canary-coloured girl, and then my relatives said things to me and about me which I simply could not stand. Remember, my father was not long dead. I was filled with unspeakable disgust. I longed to get to some other country. Why not? I had a thousand pounds. For the last ten months I have been travelling about with a maid."

"You have been living on your capital then."

"Exactly. I imagined that before I came to the end of it I should be dead, or married, or should have discovered some way of earning a livelihood."

"But, even so, you travelled with a maid. Your tastes—in dress, for instance—do not seem to me, if I may be impertinent enough to express an opinion, to be of the most economical.

"This hotel, too—and you have been here some time—is charming and most comfortable, but it is also most expensive."

"My thousand lasted better than you imagine. Jeanne, my maid, is a good girl, devoted to me and not extravagant. And I was economical at first; yes, we have seen the inside of some cheap and horrible *pensions*, Jeanne and I. But I have been here several weeks without paying anything at all—don't trouble, for it will all be paid tomorrow. I left fourteen hundred louis at the bureau before dinner."

"Then you have been gambling."

"I have. This morning my position was terrible; I could see ruin closing a lean paw on my neck. I had had hints from the hotel people—and something more than hints. I heard the gossip of the hotel servants from my faithful Jeanne. I have no valuable jewels, and I do not travel in great state. The marvel of marvels is that I have been allowed to go on so long. I had to do something this morning to restore my credit. There were the bank-notes in their case, locked away in my dressing-bag. I dared not change one of them, but I was only taking a safe precaution in leaving them with the hotel people, and they would make my credit good again. There would be no enquiry as to the numbers, unless I tried to change them. Then I went off to the rooms to play for my life, knowing that I was playing for my life. I had paid Jeanne before starting out, and I had just five louis left in my purse. You know the result—luck has never left me all day. Now that you have been so kind to me, I think the luck still holds."

"But you will not play again?"

"Never, never!"

"And these notes?"

"I wish you would be kind enough to send them back to that bank for me at once—anonymously, of course."

"You shall send them yourself, but I will address an envelope to Stanniwell & Co. for you and write an anonymous message for you to enclose with them. It will explain that the sender had nothing to do with the theft, and ask that the receipt may be acknowledged in the *Morning Post*."

"Yes. Thanks very much. You have been so good to me about this."

"Perhaps you would join me in the writing-room in five minutes. I shall have everything ready by then."

"Yes, I will come there. Oh please wait a minute! I forgot, I forgot. I have never thanked you for returning my little handkerchief."

She was most naïve and ridiculous and charming. We were all alone in the garden. I caught her in my arms, and kissed her many times, and neither of us said a word.

Later in the evening we sent off the notes to Stanniwell & Co. I had naturally thought it better that her handwriting should not appear in the matter, though there was but the slightest chance of anything being traced in that way. I may add that the unexpected restitution of the notes after this lapse of time made a considerable sensation in London. Their receipt was duly acknowledged in the way we had prescribed.

I do not know—and probably never shall know—whether George Endelwode was the actual thief, or merely a receiver, or if he had simply taken care of the notes on behalf of some friend who did not dare to claim them when George Endelwode died.

On the following morning—the morning of the day on which I write this—I asked Miss Endelwode to marry me. The wedding will be in two months' time.

I shall have but one more exploit to record. Information has reached me with regard to Lady Seaforth's jewels, and I must act upon it. But as soon as that is brought to a successful issue, I break with the past. I will be stronger than my fate.

I see the only true happiness awaiting me, and happy people have no memoirs.

XII

MURDER

When I last wrote, it was at the time of my engagement, when I had made up my mind to enter upon a new life altogether. My theft of Lady Seaforth's jewels was to be the last crime with which I was to be associated. It is so easy to make plans for the morrow, not knowing what the morrow will bring forth. That theft was not my last crime nor my worst. I write now with the certainty that my marriage will never take place, and in awful fear of imminent catastrophe.

There is really very little to say as to that theft. An attempt had been made upon Lady Seaforth's jewels sometime before by a man of bad character, whom I afterwards had the privilege of bringing back to the paths of rectitude. Lady Seaforth regularly spent part of the winter in the Riviera, and took her diamonds with her. They were carried in an ordinary morocco bag, which she kept in her own possession. Neither her own maid nor any of the servants travelling with her ever handled that bag at all. With great trouble I managed to get a sight of it, and, thanks to an excellent memory, I had had a duplicate made, which, at any rate, resembled it closely enough to be mistaken for it in a bad light. An exceptionally rough Channel passage gave me the opportunity I wanted. For her ladyship, though not ill, was not so fresh and alert as usual; it was some few hours after we reached Calais that my opportunity came. When the loss was discovered, she said—and I have no doubt that she believed—that the bag had never been out of her hand. It would not be so easy to deceive others if it were not even easier for them to deceive themselves. It always amuses an expert conjurer to hear one of his tricks described by one of the audience. The man in the audience never tells what he really saw, but only what he thought he saw, which is a very different matter. I returned to England at once and did the work of removing the stones from their setting at my house in Bloomsbury, and the settings themselves are now at the bottom of the Thames. I was in no hurry to dispose of the stones; I could very well wait until the next time that I happened to visit my friend the diamond merchant in Brussels. In the meantime the excitement about the theft would have died down. It is the want of capital, making an immediate realisation necessary, which causes so many a clever man to lose his liberty. I was in the fortunate position that I could afford to wait.

The whole transaction would have completely satisfied me but for one thing—the time when the diamonds were taken was two o'clock on Sunday morning. I have already stated my views with regard to Sunday work, and my firm conviction that if I ever transgressed in this way disaster would follow. I cannot of course explain, what some will think, the superstitious regard for one commandment, at the very moment when I was breaking another; I can only say that it was so, and that even at the moment of the theft, and powerless to resist the opportunity that was offered to me, I knew that this would end badly. Long after every trace had been removed which could have connected me with the theft of Lady Seaforth's diamonds, I still had this conviction. The fact is that I had intended to take them on Saturday night while I was on the boat, and had felt fairly certain of my ability to do so; as it happened, no opportunity presented itself then, and, once in pursuit of the prey, I was unable to leave it until it was mine.

I never lock up my diamonds.

I am interested in gardening, and the garden attached to my cottage at Brighton does me some credit. In an unlocked drawer of my writing-table, both at Brighton and at my house at Bloomsbury, I have generally got a collection of flower-seeds in different packets. These packets are labelled in the usual way with the name of the seed and directions for cultivation. You might open a score of them, taken at random from the drawer, and find the contents answer exactly to the printed description on the cover. And the twenty-first packet might enclose something far more valuable than the seed of the new mignonette with which the label credited it. It is a simple but most effective method of taking care of loose stones, and had always left me, so far as they were concerned, with no fear of burglars.

I put the diamonds which I got from Lady Seaforth into three packets. I did this work late at night when the rest of my household were in bed. About a week afterwards it was necessary for me to open one of these packets for the purpose of verifying the weight of one of the diamonds. I found that this packet was missing. Further search showed me that the other two packets were missing as well. I felt sure that my foe was one of my own household. Even then the thought of Mrs Pethwick, my housekeeper, sour and bitter at my approaching marriage and her own dismissal, crossed my mind. Yet this woman had been an honest and devoted servant for ten years or more; the thing seemed impossible. I shut the drawer containing the seeds and sat down to think. There were many courses of action open before me, and I was confident that whichever course I chose would prove wrong. I recognised that my curse had come upon me, and that I could not get away from it. I was wretchedly nervous, and it was with great difficulty that I could bring myself to act at all. Perhaps it would have been better if I had not acted at all—if I had accepted my loss as my punishment—said nothing and done nothing.

After dinner at night I went up to my library, rang, and asked if Mrs Pethwick would be good enough to speak to me for a moment. Presently she came in, neatly dressed in black as usual, and with the pleasant rather deferential smile with which I was familiar. It was, I suppose, due to the force of habit, for her expression changed when I spoke to her. It was as though she now took off her disguise for the first time. The wheel had gone round, and she, who had always received my orders with such cheerful readiness, was now in a position to dictate. And she knew it. "Mrs Pethwick," I said, "sometime ago I purchased from a dealer in Hatton Garden a quantity of diamonds, cut but unset. They were intended as my wedding present to the lady whom I am going to marry. I have, as you know, no safe in the house, and undoubtedly I should have sent them to my bankers; but it occurred to me that they would be quite secure if nobody knew that they were diamonds, and that I might spare myself the bother of going to the bank about them. I placed them in three packets purporting to contain flower-seeds, and put them in the drawer which you see open there. This afternoon I found that they were missing. You are in a position of responsibility in this house, and it is to you that I come first: do you know anything about these diamonds, can you suggest anything?"

"Certainly," she said, "I took them." She really did it extremely well. She was perfectly quiet, and had that air of not wishing to make an effect which is so immensely effective.

"You took them," I repeated.

"I took them, and in all probability shall keep them, until I get a chance of selling them." She gave a little bitter laugh. "One must have one's little compensations," she added.

"Mrs Pethwick," I said, "you have surprised me terribly. I could never have believed that you were capable of such dishonesty. However, your manner offers an explanation. You were not yourself then, and you are not yourself now; you have perhaps had some mental worry of which I know nothing; the impudence of your confession is alone proof enough that you need the care of a specialist. Meanwhile I remember your long services to me, and I shall do the best I can for you. We will speak of this no more at present, and you will do well not to let your mind dwell upon it. Tomorrow a doctor shall see you."

It is difficult when you are playing a game, which you know to be a losing game, to play it as well as you can, and this was what I was doing. I wanted to see the extent of her knowledge.

"I am not insane," she said grimly, "and you know it. You will send for no doctor, because you dare not. I have stolen your diamonds—do you understand that? And the law gives you your remedy, and you dare not take that either!"

This had the disadvantage, from my point of view, of being absolutely true. "Very well," I said, "these are extraordinary statements. Perhaps you will tell me what you mean by them. You can sit down, if you like."

She sat down, there was no trace of excitement in her manner. A person who holds all the trump cards has no need to be excited. "I may say," she said, "that I have known the secret of your double life for some time past. I have kept the secret, and until now have made no use of it; but you have told me of your approaching marriage. I am not an old woman yet, but I am growing old, and I was to be flung aside. But not now—now I dictate my own terms."

"Will you," I said, "be good enough to tell me how you have discovered what in your slightly transpontine way you call the secret of my double life? By the way, it might also be interesting to know what this supposed double life is."

I could not succeed in annoying her in the least.

"Certainly," she said. "You who have preached to others are a thief; the diamonds which I took from you are those which you stole from Lady Seaforth. How do I know these things?" She paused and then spoke with more vehemence. "Yes, you have been very clever, that is true enough. You have outwitted the police, outwitted everybody but myself; you forgot me, you see. I will do you the justice to say that you are not a vain man. The possibility of a woman being"—she hesitated for her word— "interested in you as I have been never occurred to you. I was little more than a servant, and if I was not old I was certainly no longer young. Never mind all that; you don't want to know it. It is enough for you to know that I have watched and questioned. I know why, for instance, when you leave on your motor-car for Brighton you are so late in arriving there."

"Really? You are wonderful; you even find out secrets where there are none. Why don't you invent a motor tyre that cannot puncture? It would save your suspicions and confessions, and, incidentally, your self-respect."

And still she would not be angry. If I could have driven her into a blind fury and made her lose her head, I might yet have been able to save the situation; as it was, it seemed to me that I had but the choice of two things.

"Let me go on," she continued quietly. "Relying on the scrupulous honesty of your household and on your belief that nobody could suspect a gentleman in your position, you have been very careless. You have been careless with your keys; I have had a complete set of duplicates made. You have been careless, too, with your blotting-paper. The man who writes the long memoirs that you write these long winter evenings after dinner, should be particularly careful about his blotting-paper; it is so easy with a looking-glass, you know. It is easy enough, too, when one turns over a packet of seeds to find what one has hunted the whole house for, to notice that these seeds are different sizes and of the wrong weight, and unusually hard. It was all too simple and childish for you to trouble about; you doubted, probably, whether I had any intelligence at all, apart from housekeeping. I have watched you in a thousand ways — yes, and I have saved you from discovery before this. A woman is satisfied with very little, you know, and I had that little. Now you take that away. Very well, I will rob you first, and I will ruin you afterwards."

I passed the tip of my tongue over my lips, when I spoke my voice had become husky. "So you have kept my secret until now?" I said.

"Oh yes," she said bitterly, "and I have been fool enough to let you know why. You cannot marry me, of course. I do not think under any circumstances I would have married you; but most certainly you shall marry no one else. Does that sound unreasonable to you?"

"If you don't mind," I said, "I should like a little time to think this over. I have nearly decided what to do, and I admit that you are too strong for me. But the question is a momentous one. Come to me again at ten tonight."

She rose from her chair; her manner changed abruptly, there was no longer a trace of a threat in it, it was again almost deferential. "I see, sir," she said, "that you are much upset. It sounds queer, but I really am sorry to have given you this trouble. Why, I have spent the last seven years of my life in trying to the utmost of my power to save you trouble of every kind. True, I have been paid for it; but my services have not been those for which one can very well pay. Yes, several times, though you never knew it, I have stood between you and discovery; perhaps I shall tell you all about it one of these days. Well, well, I will wait until ten o'clock." She gave a little bitter laugh. "I am used to waiting," she said, and without another word she went out.

It was exactly nine o'clock; I had just one hour in which to think and to act. Mrs Pethwick had changed little in appearance in the last seven years, but I saw her tonight with new eyes; the mask had fallen, and the real woman had shown herself. I had seen those submissive eyes lit up with passion. I had heard that carefully modulated voice grow harsh and raucous. Yes, I suppose she had been a handsome woman once; I had never cared to have quite ugly people about me. And with her tonight, it was to be one of two things.

There was a third course open, that I should give up my marriage and go on living in this house as before. But I put that aside at once: I should still be entirely in the hands of Mrs Pethwick; one day she might change her mind; it was impossible to say what a woman in that position would not do—it was not to be thought of for a moment. Only under two conditions could I feel absolutely confident. One was that I should give her my name, and take her into partnership with me in every way. I thought this over a long time, utterly absorbed in it, and finally rejected it. It asked too much. Therefore only one thing was left, and that thing was horrible. I blamed her for it; she was a fool; she had brought it upon herself; she should have known that it would have been impossible for me to let her go on living after this. I glanced at my watch; it was five-and-twenty minutes to ten. I had made up my mind, but there was still much to do, and it had to be done quickly.

In a little cabinet in the library I keep various liquors and glasses. I have found the arrangement useful, for sometimes when I am alone my nerves have been unable to stand it any longer, and I have wished, without the knowledge of any other person in the house, to get intoxicated. From this cabinet I now took a bottle of champagne. Mrs Pethwick, I guessed, would know me desperate and would be ready to suspect me of everything; but she would not believe that a bottle of champagne could be opened, and tampered with, and then recorked in such a way as to leave no sign. It is really quite a simple operation, when one knows the exact right way to do it. I had practised it before. I had always thought it a thing that might one day be useful. I opened the bottle, made a slight addition to the contents, and then replaced the cork, the string, the wire, and the gilt foil just as before. I knew that the foil might not be thoroughly dry by ten o'clock, but in all probability it would not be until an hour later that I should want it. The table in the middle of my room is covered with a cloth, which hangs down for about eighteen inches all round; to one of the legs of this table, in such a position that it would be hidden by the cloth, I fixed a little shelf. It was the simplest possible arrangement, made with the lid of a cigar box. I filled a glass from another bottle of champagne and placed this on the shelf. It would be necessary for me to drink with Mrs Pethwick, and not to drink the wine she poured out for me. My mind was perfectly clear now, and I had thought out the minutest detail. The champagne in the glass on the shelf would be flat and still when the moment came for me to change it for the glass from which it was not safe for me to drink. Probably Mrs Pethwick would not notice this detail, but in any case I was ready. I had a pinch of sugar to add to the glass at the last moment. I drew my chair near to that leg of the table in which the shelf was placed, and waited. It was now three minutes to ten, and it seemed ages before I heard Mrs Pethwick's gentle tap at the door. Yet she was exactly punctual, as she always was.

It was a delicate business; if the woman had been quite a fool it would have been much easier, but in some ways I had at present a high opinion of Mrs Pethwick's sharpness. It has always been a cardinal principle with me never to tell an unnecessary lie. It was necessary that I should say that I had given up all thoughts of marriage, and that she should herself see the letter which I would write in the morning to break off my engagement. That was the inevitable lie. But I was speaking the sober truth when I told her that it touched me deeply that she, knowing exactly what I was and how utterly unworthy I was of her, or any woman, should still care for me. I was not only touched but pleased; a few hours before, I might have agreed with Mrs Pethwick that I was not a vain man, yet now through all my mental tumult, through my terror at what had been discovered, and through my horror of what I had yet to do, the voice of vanity made itself heard. I could imagine myself grinning like a flattered school-boy. From this point I went on by slow degrees with her. I broached the idea of a partnership: we should work together, nominally she would remain my housekeeper; in reality she would share in the proceeds of every exploit, and possibly in the execution of many of them. I told her that I had often thought that I could do more if I had a woman accomplice whom I could trust absolutely. That was quite true.

"If you wish that," she said, "it shall be so. I have never stolen anything in my life except those diamonds, and it was not chiefly for their value that I took them. I was well brought up; I was taught to hate dishonesty, and I do hate it, but that shall all go for you, if you say so. If you wanted me to burn my right hand off for you, or to lose my soul for you, it would have to be."

It chanced that at this moment the flame of my lamp began to smoke a little. She noticed it at once and turned it down; she was an excellent housekeeper. The trouble was that she was a woman as well.

I began to speak of religious matters; I told her that it seemed to me that she was a fatalist and that I had been a fatalist too. I told her how in my early days I had struggled to let the good in me prevail over the bad; and how the struggle had been given up in the firm conviction that I was to save the souls of others but inevitably to lose my own. I spoke to her with fervour, saying what I felt deeply and carried away, as I always am, by my own words. When I had finished there were tears in her eyes. Yet all the time I had been listening intently, with a hearing that long practice has made wonderfully acute: I heard now what I had been waiting for—the steps of the rest of my household going up to bed.

"Is it too late?" she said. "Had you married you would probably have given up this life. Even without that, can nothing be done?"

"It might be," I said. I spoke of the possibility of a partnership of another kind with her—a partnership not in evil but in good. I made her talk. I had thought that I should have trouble in spinning the thing out, but words came readily to both of us; and all the time, I was as much in earnest as if I had not been playing a part. It was after eleven when I found my chance to say that until tonight I had never thought of marrying, and that she had said that she would never marry me, but that one did not know what the end would be. And then, since the gradations must be gradual from the discussion of fatalism to the proposition of champagne, I made her talk of her past life and her early training. It was quite simple to dwell a little on the lighter side of that; so that it did not seem unnatural when she rose to go and I said that we must first drink together. It seemed even to mark my acceptance of the difference that had sprung up in the relations between us; it seemed a delicate way of telling her that she was to be in all ways my equal now.

How could she suspect? She herself took the wine and the glasses from the cabinet and opened the bottle. She filled the glasses, and then hesitated. "Wait one moment," she said. "I must first give these back to you."

She took the diamonds, still in the packets where I had placed them, from the bag which she carried at her waist, and handed them to me. I took them and began to say how difficult it was for me to speak, that I felt dazed and could not express what I thought As I spoke I dropped one of the packets; I stooped to pick it up with the glass of champagne which she had poured out for me still in my hand. The opportunity was made for me. I left that glass on the floor. When I rose I held in my hand the glass which unobserved I had taken from the shelf. We drank, and then it was time for me to hurry her off, for the thing that I had given her works quickly, and I did not want to watch the coming of the end. I shook hands with her as I said good-night. I waited for an hour, of which but a few minutes were occupied in planning what was to be done next. It was all over, and it was of no good to think about it now. I took down a volume of Matthew Arnold's, his "Literature and Dogma," and read to occupy my mind. At the end of the hour I went as softly as possible up to her room. My key opened the door. In the room Mrs Pethwick lay on her bed fully dressed under the bright gas-jet. There was an open Bible by her side, with pencil annotations in the margin. The body turned over as I touched it. She was quite dead. I was surprised to find how quiet and how little moved I was now. I closed the Bible and put it back on the table by her bed-side; then I picked up the body—a singularly awkward thing to carry—and took it down to the room where we had been sitting. Then I went back to her room and turned out the gas. There was no particular reason why I should have done this; it almost amused me that one's careful habit of avoiding waste should survive even in such a time of stress. When I had got down to my own room again I put the body behind the screen. So far my nerves had been steady enough; I was afraid that the continued sight of the thing might break me down. I poured the poisoned champagne away, washed the bottle carefully, and then put into it a little wine from the second bottle that I had opened. I finished the remainder of the second bottle.

My motor-car is kept in the coach-house, and I now went down and ran it out, taking care to make as little noise as possible. As I lit the lamps, I was glad to notice that the man whom I employed to clean it had neglected it that night, and consequently I should not have the bother of cleaning it myself when I got back in the early hours, for the man would have no suspicion that the car had been taken out. I left it outside my front door and went into the house; I put on my own overcoat and cap, collected the things that I wanted for the part of the work that I dreaded most, and went back to the room where the body lay. I should not have been surprised if, as I opened the door, I had seen Mrs Pethwick's eyes staring out at me from above the screen. I should not have been surprised if I had found nothing behind the screen and had suddenly awakened to find that this was all a dream. But the body was there just as I had left it; the thing had been done which nothing can ever alter. I dressed it in an old ulster and cap of my own. A neck wrap hid the hair. The last horrible touch was to add a false beard. I carried the body down to the hall-door and peered out. So far as I could see, the street was empty. As quickly as I could I rushed down the steps to the car with the body. The rest was all simple enough; I put the rug round it, hiding the hands that looked so horribly white, and tied it into its position. I had stepped down from the car, and was making my final arrangements for starting when a policeman came round the corner. I knew the man. He looked at me and at the thing in the car and said good-night. I could not make out whether he suspected anything or not. I was terribly afraid that he might speak to the dead body, and I was careful to stand between him and it. "Good-night," I replied cheerfully. "My friend here thought it would be a nice night for a spin, else I am not often as late as this." He said something about the roads being pretty clear anyhow, and walked on. I could not say that he suspected, but he had certainly noticed. I had hoped that I might get away from my house without being seen, but as this was not to be I could only make the best of it. A half turn of the handle and my engine started; in another moment we were off, the dead body and I. Nothing that I could do would keep that head from shaking.

I left the body in a copse on Wimbledon Common, covering it with bracken and bringing back the disguise with me. Before going to bed I possessed myself of Mrs Pethwick's set of the duplicates of my keys, and destroyed the false beard in the fire. Then I took a bottle of brandy up to my room, but this night I could neither get drunk nor could I sleep; all the time my hands seemed to be clinging to the steering-wheel, and from the corner of my eye, I still saw the head of the dead woman, made grotesque by the false beard, nodding in languorous imbecility. I rose early and wrote this account. Almost all day I have felt strangely cold, and have sat cowering over the fire. My servants are in the state of the wildest excitement about the mysterious disappearance of Mrs Pethwick. I had of course to go to the police station to make enquiries. I did it very badly. An inspector asked me if I was ill. I said that this business had naturally upset me a good deal; he looked at me queerly. Everybody looks at me queerly now, almost as if they saw the brand on my forehead.

I add this note two days later. This is the end. The body has been found and identified; the policeman who saw me in the motor-car has told what he saw. They are watching my house;

I can see them from this window. Every moment I expect them to come and take me. I might have got clear away; I might even now, if I had the head for it, manage to show that there was no evidence against me. But I know that it is written that this shall be the end. More evidence will come; it is useless to prolong the struggle.

But they will not take me alive. I still keep that last cigarette, and they will hardly refuse me permission to smoke it on my way to the station. That lesson in high explosives will be given after all.

And so I close the book of my life.

THE END

Yellowback range available...

1. The Old Man in the Corner by Orczy, Baroness Emma
2. The Complete Max Carrados Vol 1 by Bramah, Ernest
3. The Complete Max Carrados Vol 2 by Bramah, Ernest

THE ARSÈNE LUPIN SERIES BY LEBLANC, MAURICE:

4. Arsène Lupin 1: The Extraordinary Adventures of Arsène Lupin - Gentleman Burglar
5. Arsène Lupin 2: Arsène Lupin vs. Herlock Sholmes
6. Arsène Lupin 3. The Hollow Needle
7. Arsène Lupin 4: 813
8. Arsène Lupin 5: The Crystal Stopper
9. Arsène Lupin 6: The Confessions of Arsène Lupin
10. Arsène Lupin 7: The Teeth of the Tiger
11. Arsène Lupin 8: The Shell Shard (aka The Woman of Mystery)
12. Arsène Lupin 9: The Return of Arsène Lupin (aka The Golden Triangle)
13. Arsène Lupin 10: The secret of Sarek (aka Island of Thirty Coffins)
14. Arsène Lupin 11: The Eight Strokes of the Clock
15. Arsène Lupin 12: The Secret Tomb
16. Arsène Lupin 13: The Countess of Cagliostro (aka Memoirs of Arsène Lupin)
17. Arsène Lupin (bonus book): Arsène Lupin (novelised by Edgar Jepson from LeBlanc's original play)

18. The Complete Raffles by Hornung, E. W.
19. The Mysterious Mickey Finn by Paul, Eliott
20. You Play the Black and the Red Comes Up by Hallas, Richard
21. The Mr. Moto Omnibus Vol 1 by Marquand, John P.
22. The Mr. Moto Omnibus Vol 2 by Marquand, John P.
23. The Complete Father Brown Vol 1 (with original illustrations) by Chesterton, G. K.
24. The Complete Father Brown Vol 2 (with original illustrations) by Chesterton, G. K.
25. A Peter Wimsey omnibus: Murder Must Advertise & The Nine Tailors by Sayers, Dorothy L.
26. Was it Murder? by Hilton, James
27. The Complete Just Men Volume 1 by Wallace, Edgar
28. The Complete Just Men Volume 2 by Wallace, Edgar
29. Carnacki by Hodgson, William Hope
30. Grey Mask by Wentworth, Patricia
31. The Case With Nine Solutions by Connington, J. J.
32. Murder by Matchlight by Lorac, E. C. R.
33. The Crossword Mystery by Punshon, E. R.
34. The Cask by Crofts, Freeman Wills
35. The Bells of Old Bailey by Bowers, Dorothy
36. Crime Unlimited by Hume, David
37. The A. A. Milne Mystery Omnibus (contains: The Red house and Four days' wonder) by Milne, A. A.
38. She Faded into Air by White, Ethel Lina
39. The Wheel Spins by White, Ethel Lina
40. The Spiral Staircase by White, Ethel Lina
41. Murder of a Lady by Wynne, Anthony
42. Thirteen Guests by Farjeon, J. Jefferson
43. The Daughter of Time by Tey, Josephine
44. The Man in the Queue by Tey, Josephine
45. A Shilling for Candles by Tey, Josephine
46. The Franchise Affair by Tey, Josephine
47. Tragedy at Law by Hare, Cyril
48. The Moonstone by Collins, Wilkie
49. The Woman in White by Collins, Wilkie
50. The Circular Staircase by Rinehart, Mary Roberts
51. The Benson Murder Case by Van Dine, S. S.
52. The Philip Marlowe Omnibus by Chandler, Raymond
53. Monsieur Lecoq by Gaboriau, Emile
54. Aurora Floyd by Braddon, Mary Elizabeth
55. The Big Bow Mystery by Zangwill, Israel
56. Dossier 113 (aka The Blackmailers) by Gaboriau, Emile
57. The Mystery of a Hansom Cab by Hume, Fergus
58. The W Plan by Seton, Graham
59. Inspector French's Greatest Case by Crofts, Freeman Wills

60. Mr Bowling Buys a Newspaper by Henderson, Donald
61. A Voice Like Velvet by Henderson, Donald
62. The Deductions of Colonel Gore by Brock, Lynn
63. The Rogue's Syndicate by Froest, Frank
64. The Middle Temple Murder by Fletcher, J. S.
65. The Millionaire Mystery by Hume, Fergus
66. Below the Clock by Turner, J. V.
67. The Rouletabille Omnibus: The Mystery of the Yellow Room and The Perfume of the Lady in Black by Leroux, Gaston
68. The Complete Dupin by Poe, Edgar Allan
69. The Complete Thinking Machine Vol 1 by Futrelle, Jacques
70. The Complete Thinking Machine Vol 2 by Futrelle, Jacques
71. The Complete Thinking Machine Vol 3 by Futrelle, Jacques
72. The Complete Montague Egg by Sayers, Dorothy L.
73. The Complete J. G. Reeder by Wallace, Edgar
74. The Complete Charlie Chan Vol 1 by Biggers, Earl der
75. The Complete Charlie Chan Vol 2 by Biggers, Earl der
76. The Dr Nikola Omnibus Vol 1 by Boothby, Guy
77. The Dr Nikola Omnibus Vol 2 by Boothby, Guy
78. A Prince of Swindlers: The Simon Carne collection by Boothby, Guy
79. The Slim Callaghan Omnibus by Cheyney, Peter
80. The Fu Manchu Omnibus by Rohmer, Sax
81. The Bulldog Drummond Omnibus: The Complete Peterson Rounds by Sapper
82. The Avenging Ray by Seamark
83. The Richard Chandos Omnibus by Yates, Dornford
84. The Alan Quatermain Omnibus: King Solomon's Mines & Allan Quatermain by Haggard, H. Rider
85. The 39 steps by Buchan, John
86. At The Villa Rose by Mason, A.E.W.
87. The Eye of Osiris by Freeman, R. Austin
88. The Weapons of Mystery by Hocking, Joseph
89. The House of Dr. Edwardes by Beeding, Francis
90. The Seven Secrets by Le Queux, William
91. Call Mr Fortune by Bailey, H. C.
92. The Three Taps by Knox, Ronald
93. The Girl at Central by Bonner, Geraldine
94. The Experiences of Loveday Brooke, Lady Detective by Pirkis, Catherine Louisa
95. Mary Louise by Baum, L. Frank
96. That Affair Next Door by Green, Anna Katherine
97. Dead Letter by Regester, Seeley
98. The Tragedy of Pudd'nhead Wilson by Twain, Mark
99. The Big Clock by Fearing, Kenneth
100. The Woman in the Window by Wallis, J. H.
101. The Sexton Blake Collection Vol 1 by Hal Meredeth (or many?)
102. The Complete Simon Iff Stories by Crowley, Aleister
103. The Castle of Otranto by Walpole, Horace
104. The Adventures of the Infallible Godahl by Anderson, Frederick Irving

THE COMPLETE SHERLOCK HOLMES
105. A Study In Scarlet
106. The Sign Of Four
107. The Adventures Of Sherlock Holmes
108. The Memoirs Of Sherlock Holmes
109. The Hound Of The Baskervilles
110. The Return Of Sherlock Holmes
111. His Last Bow
112. The Valley Of Fear
113. The Case-Book Of Sherlock Holmes

114. Graustark: The Story of a Love Behind a Throne by George Barr McCutcheon
115. Beverly of Graustark by George Barr McCutcheon
116. Truxton King: A Story of Graustark by George Barr McCutcheon
117. The Prince of Graustark by George Barr McCutcheon
118. The Complete Zenda Omnibus by Anthony Hope
119. The Mad king by Burroughs, Edgar Rice
120. The Fantomas Omnibus by Souvestre, Pierre

121. The Problemist by Clinton H. Stagg
122. The Dorrington Deed-Box by Morrison, Arthur
123. The Lone Wolf by Vance, L. J.
124. The Complete Martin Hewitt Collection Vol 1: Martin Hewitt, Investigator & Chronicles of Martin Hewitt by Morrison, Arthur
125. The Complete Martin Hewitt Collection Vol 2: Adventures of Martin Hewitt & The Red Triangle: Further Chronicles of Martin Hewitt by Morrison, Arthur
126. Seven Keys to Baldpate by Earl Derr Biggers
127. No Pockets in a Shroud by McCoy, Horace
128. The John Silence Collection by Blackwood, Algernon
129. Lady Molly Of Scotland Yard by Orczy, Baroness Emma
130. Skin O' My Tooth by Orczy, Baroness Emma
131. The Wrong Box by Stevenson, R. L. and Lloyd Osbourne
132. Tutt and Mr Tutt by Train, Arthur C.
133. The Clue by Wells, Carolyn
134. The Complete Trent Case Book by Bentley, E. C.
135. The Luck of the Vails by Benson, E. F.
136. The Rome Express by Griffiths, Arthur
137. The Complete Curious Mr Tarrant by C. Daly King
138. Rope and Gaslight (2-in-1 text) by Hamilton, Patrick
139. Prince Zaleski and Cumming's King Monk by Shiel, M. P.
140. The Assassination Bureau Ltd. by London, Jack
141. Introducing Clubfoot by Williams, Valentine
142. Master of Mysteries: The complete Uncle Abner collection by Post, Melville Davisson
143. The Red Redmaynes by Phillpotts, Eden
144. Thrilling Stories of the Railway by Whitechurch, Victor L.
145. The Grey Wig: Stories and Novelettes by Zangwill, Israel
146. The Lodger by Lowndes, Marie Belloc
147. The Man from Manchester by Donovan, Dick (Joyce Emerson Preston Muddock)
148. Mr. Meeson's Will by H. Rider Haggard by Haggard, H. Rider
149. Devlin the Barber by Farjeon, B. L.
150. Checkmate by Joseph Sheridan Le Fanu
151. Recollections of a Detective Police-Officer by Waters
152. The Widow Lerouge by Gaboriau, Emile
153. The Expressman and the Detective by Pinkerton, Allan
154. Zadig and Vathek by Voltaire
155. The Stillwater Tragedy by Aldrich, Thomas Bailey
156. The Memoirs of Constantine Dix by Pain, Barry
157. Ashes to Ashes by Ostrander, Isabel
158. The Jewel of Seven Stars by Stoker, Bram
159. The Thomas Love Peacock Collection by Peacock, Thomas Love

THE COMPLETE DERLETH SOLAR PONS

160. In Re: Sherlock Holmes - The Adventures of Solar Pons
161. The Memoirs of Solar Pons
162. The Return of Solar Pons
163. The Reminiscences of Solar Pons
164. The Casebook of Solar Pons
165. The Novels of Solar Pons: Terror over London and Mr. Fairlie's Final Journey
166. The Chronicles of Solar Pons
167. The Apocrypha of Solar Pons

168. The Triumphs of Eugene Valmont
169. The Female Detective by Forrester, Andrew
170. Cain's Jawbone by Torquemada
171. The Great Impersonation by Oppenheim, E. Phillips

THE DASHIELL HAMMETT COLLECTION

172. The Complete Sam Spade
173. The Complete Thin Man
174. The Complete Continental Op Vol 1
175. The Complete Continental Op Vol 2

All books may not be available in all territories due to rights restrictions.

For more details and a full list of titles visit https://www.hachetteindia.com/home/yellowbacks

A fan of Sherlock Holmes?
Then meet Solar Pons

The original fan fiction from the great August Derleth—the Sherlock Holmes of Praed Street.

"the best substitutes for Sherlock Holmes known."
– Vincent Starrett

"an excellent series of adventures in detection in their own right." – *The Chicago Tribune*

For more details and a full list of titles:
visit https://www.hachetteindia.com/home/yellowbacks